BEFORE THE EIGHTH

SANIYA SAHEER

Notion Press Media Pvt Ltd

No. 50, Chettiyar Agaram Main Road,
Vanagaram, Chennai, Tamil Nadu – 600 095

First Published by Notion Press 2022
Copyright © Saniya Saheer 2022
All Rights Reserved.

ISBN 979-8-88530-469-6

AUTHOR'S NOTE

Thank you.

To my sisters, Vandana Krishna and Salma Saheer, who have been the dearest people to me and this book.

I love you both so very much.

To Agaatha Antony, who has been the most supportive friend anyone could ask for. I consider myself lucky to have you.

To Archit Ameya, for all the effort you put and the confidence you instilled. I don't have enough words to express my love and gratitude for you.

To Parvathy Vivek, for motivating me with the bursting positivity you own. I am extremely grateful to have you.

And finally, to my parents, Sheeba and Saheer, without whom this wouldn't have been possible. I love you both beyond words.

Once again, thank you.

To the fantasies we weave and the demons we let lose.

To Vandana and Salma,

This is ours.

PROLOGUE

"If this is how it is meant to end, then it should end that way. It is what it is Sam."

Screams. Vivid visions. Cries. Shock. I woke up covered in sweat, frantically looking around to make sure I was safe. Of course, I was safe. I wanted so badly to make myself believe that things were not the way it was, that all of it was just a nightmare. But as if to prove me wrong, the black tuxedo that hung on my wardrobe door laughed mockingly at me. It was true and it will always be. I looked outside at the rain that was splattering on my window and thought about how my life had changed and how I had changed.

You could maybe call this a tale of valor, of friendship, of hope, of strength. But, above all, this is a tale of loss and death.

PART ONE

"Memory runs her needle in and out, up and down, hither and thither.

We know not what comes next, or what follows after."

– Virginia Wolf.

CHAPTER ONE

I hate mornings. That much I knew as I got up from the bed, pushing the sheets away from me, stretching my hands and legs. Sunshine seeped into my room as I pulled the curtains apart and stared down the alley. I lived in B21 Street, in the northernmost side of Waltunor, a small city in the vast geography of Scotland. I have lived here my entire life and I knew this place more than I know myself. Even though I know almost all of the small population of 10,402 people, hardly anyone knew me. So much for being an introvert, I guess.

I picked up random clothes to wear, still half asleep. I could see mom's huddled figure near the kitchen counter as I descended the steps towards the dining. "Good morning." she wished as she added some toast and scrambled eggs onto my plate. "Brianna, come down here or you are going to be late."

"I am already here mom", a listless voice replied, hurriedly sliding onto the seat beside me.

Brianna was just a year younger than me, but our similarities ended with dad's bright blue eyes and mom's straight black hair; we were poles apart in everything else. She was easily one of the most popular girls in our school, God knows how. She was Brianna and I was Brianna's brother.

"Aren't you guys late today?" dad asked as he made his way towards the front door. Brianna and I simultaneously glanced at the clock and cursed, me under my breath and Brianna on top of her voice.

"Language!" my mom rolled her eyes. I grabbed my keys, muttered goodbyes and walked out of the front door, my eyes, for a moment, lingering questioningly on Brianna who still sat there eating breakfast.

As I drove my way towards Dawin High School, listening to the silence that engulfed me, I knew that I wouldn't trade this tiny community for any other place. Waltunor was small, calm and beautiful and this is exactly where I belonged. As I entered school, I spotted a few familiar faces of people whom I shared classes with or people who lived nearby. Some waved at me and I smiled back. I parked my bike, slanged my backpack onto my shoulder and walked towards the main doors. The school was a dirty white, old building that stood correctly in the center of our town, being a sign between the crowded side of Waltunor and the silent living quarters.

"Sam" I turned around to find Morgan walking towards me. Morgan Connor was my only friend; in fact, my girlfriend.

"Hey"; she said approaching me, "Why are you looking at me like that?"

"You look good." She was wearing a loose grey t-shirt and light blue jeans, a casual thing to wear, but she looked pretty. Her wavy brown hair was tied back in a ponytail and her t-shirt complemented her bright green eyes.

Her dark red lips widened into a smile and she said, "I always do."

We walked through the corridor, pushing through the morning traffic and trying to find our way towards our lockers. From all the lockers that the whole school had, Morgan's was the simplest one - no stickers, no posters, no hangings, nothing. Even my locker's inside held a picture of my family and some random posters of books I loved. Morgan was that kind of person who did not believe in anything that did not make sense and sticking posters or decorating one's locker was definitely on her list. It was in the biology lab that I had met her for the first time. And it wasn't her green eyes or her pretty smile that caught my attention; it was something she said: "We study all of this, life springing up from a microscopic cell and death coming from the same microscopic cell, yet here we are, saying that life cannot be explained by anyone else other than God. By the way, where is he?" I had looked at her and since then I had not stopped paying attention. And today when I looked at her again, I saw the same person, strong and stubborn. We parted ways now, at the bottom of the stairs as I headed up for History and she went off for French.

*****

"So Scotland is known for its vast and interesting history and our place, Waltunor, is a visual representation of this. So now I will divide the class into groups and your job is to find a particular place here, in Waltunor and study about its history, myths, culture, architecture and all that you can find about it". Mr.Beckham leaned over the desk, his hands bearing his body's weight. "This assignment is essential and important for your grades, so don't take it lightly. I am going off for a break and won't be here for a while, so you all have time to do this till I return."

A group assignment, talking to new people, hanging out with new people - wow, sounds terrible! I sat there, looking around the class as Mr. Beckham called people into groups and honestly, no one seemed very enthusiastic about it. Finally I heard him call my name and walked into the midst of a bunch of unknown faces. They all looked wistfully at their friends in other groups, one of the boys grumbling under his breath.

"So you may start your discussion when you have time. Hope you find this interesting"; Mr. Beckham said at the end of the class as he gathered his books and walked out.

"Interesting? Does he even hear what he is saying?" grumbled a boy next to me. He had bright red hair and smelled strongly of dog food.

"Yeah, he is nuts." I agreed with him, happy that he started the conversation, even though I highly doubt that it was more of a thought said out loud. "I am sorry but can I know your name?"

"Evan Miles. And you are..?" Yes, I knew him, not personally but I had seen him around.

"Samuel Colton." I replied. Miles looked around at our group and asked, "Do you guys mind introducing yourselves because I don't know who you all are." Very diplomatic, I see.

The girl who sat beside me shrugged. "As if *we* know who *you* are." As a matter of fact, I did know who Miles was but I didn't say anything. She stretched her hand out towards him. "Hi I am Muriel Payton.".

We all introduced each other. The other two in my group was a boy named Aiden Hunter, who I shared Math class with, and a girl named Layla Becket, who I had seen in the hallways before but have never talked to.

"So when are we going to do this?" Layla asked in her strong Scottish accent.

"Why don't we meet tomorrow at Brim's café?" asked the Payton girl. The Brim's café is a major hangout place for most of the kids from our school and we decided that we meet there at Eleven tomorrow. After that we all went away, each of them to their friends, so I walked back alone to find Morgan. She was standing near a group of people, her brown hair visible among all the heads. I stood there hesitating to go into the group but then I saw her face, flushed red with anger. I moved over to her and as I got closer, I could hear her shouting… "Who are you to judge me, huh? Well, have you seen this so called superpower?! I haven't, so I don't believe in it. And nothing, NOTHING, you say can change my perspective."

The girl she was shouting at shook her head as if in pity, "If you don't believe what I say, you will, soon."

"That's enough." I said to the girl, grabbing hold of Morgan's hand and pulling her away from the crowd. "Morgan…"

"Save the lecture." She cut through me, her face all set. I smiled at the floor. I was not against her decisions or her beliefs; I am not much of a believer either. But today, after listening to what that girl said, a silent fear rose in me for no particular reason.

CHAPTER 2

After class Morgan and I went over to her house. Well, house was a bit of an understatement. It was a two storied mansion with chandeliers and fancy carpets, a total of seven rooms and a garden in the back facing the river Fleei's(The only river that flows through Waltunor) north bank. The house had a ring of sadness to it and I always felt that if not for Morgan's presence, it would have no cheer about it. As we entered, we saw her dad who was working on his laptop. We talked to him for a while and then went towards the garden, the size of a mini football field, settled down for some pizza and vast conversations. It was nice talking to her, partly because it was interesting to hear and partly because she does most of the talking. Seeing her talk, I thought for the hundredth time, how she ended up with me.

By evening, I got up to leave.

"Hey do you have plans tomorrow? There is an art show near our school, you want to come?"

"Oh I have a history assignment to do, a group project. We are meeting at Brim's tomorrow. Sorry." I said.

"That's cool, I'll go." She said, waving at me as I rode off, humming a tune under my breath. "Where is mom and dad?" I asked Brianna, who shook her head, as I closed the door behind me. She lay there, spread across the couch, sipping something from a plastic cup. I pushed her legs away and sat down beside her.

"Sam, there is an art show near our school tomorrow. You want to come?" she asked.

"What happened to the famous Brianna Colton? No one to accompany her?" She blew raspberry at me and then said. "Many of my friends are willing to come but they are not very…artistic. It can kind of get frustrating."

"Well… I have an assignment to do so I am not free. But Morgan is going, you can go with her." I suggested.

"Oh yeah? Way better", she said. Morgan and Brianna clicked, maybe because they were similar in a lot of aspects. I did not tell my family about Morgan for a while but if you have a sister who studies in the same school, then things are not easy to hide. Plus being Morgan's boyfriend was like being a lead star in a movie, way too much popularity. But my family welcomed Morgan whole heartedly, maybe because she was so easily loveable and the least like me.

I sat there with Brianna, she talking all about her day and me listening intently. I thought about how we used to be, years ago when I was small and she was smaller and how I used to tell her all about my day and she used to listen, wide-eyed and open mouthed. The tables had turned quite a lot.

*****

As soon as I walked into Brim's café, the smell of coffee and hot croissants filled my nostrils and my eyes swept over the place trying to find someone I met yesterday. I soon spotted the red hair among the blond and black that filled the café. It was Evan Miles, no mistake. He was popular in school, partly because he was from a famous, even royal Scottish family and mostly because of his infamous short temper. He was the center of all fights, the eye of the tornado, but not so calm.

"Hey, so no one else showed up?" I asked as I sat down opposite him.

"Don't know, just came here like…two minutes ago." He replied. "You want to order something?"

"No, let the others come." I said, noticing that there was still some smell of dog food on him. We sat there for a while, cursing Mr.Beckham and his weird ideas as one of the girls from our group came over to us. Layla Becket. She was beautiful, with straight brown hair that touched her waist and deep set hazel eyes. She just smiled and replied politely to our questions and I thankfully left Evan to do all the talking. I remembered that I had seen her around a couple of times before, but my attention had mostly been driven to the girl with partially pink colored hair who always accompanied her. Soon the door opened again and a gush of cold air blew in. I looked around and found Payton walking towards us. She wore a plain black shirt and jeans, her hair in a loose bun. She looked pretty except for one thing- a bright red scarf she wore around her neck. She smiled at us as she sat near me, shoving her bag beneath the table.

"Oh my god!" said Evan, looking at Payton.

"What?" she asked, raising an eyebrow.

"What is that?" he asked, pointing at her scarf. When I looked closely, I saw that it had pictures of black and white horses running around. I wanted to laugh, but then saw her face and thought better of it.

"I know, okay!" She said removing the scarf and tying it to one of the straps of her bag. "So are we all here?"

"No, Hunter is left." Layla said. Just as she said it, Aiden walked in through the door and sat beside Layla, muttering quick apologies for being late.

"So any ideas people...? What about you Payton?" asked Evan.

"Call me Muriel...I hate it when people address me by my last name." she said, rolling her eyes. "Why don't you guys think about something while I get us something to eat?" she got up and asked what we all wanted and went over to order.

"Well... I have been thinking and there is a place that's not likely to be chosen by anyone" Layla said; "It's the La Iglesia de Muerta por Dentro."

"The... what?" Evan asked.

"La Iglesia de Muerta por Dentro. It's this abandoned church on the far end of the city. It was once believed that demonic worship took place there and that people feared it would spread, so they blew the place to bits. Its remains are still there and there are a lot of explanations and ideas about it on the internet too." She finished.

"Demonic worship?" asked Aiden, looking uneasy.

"Which sounds cool." Muriel said, as she sat down with a tray full of coffees and sandwiches, although I had ordered a croissant. "Aiden, you really believe in this? That's totally made, just a whole bunch of nonsense." Seeing that this conversation might lead to something else, (I have experience) I spoke up, "Ok that sounds like a good place. Shall we go there?" We finished our sandwiches (Although I had ordered a croissant) and followed Layla on our own bikes towards this so called ancient place.

*****

It was a pleasant morning, the sun shining bright and clear but not very hot. We rode for a long while to reach this church and after about 30 minutes, through twists and turns and almost covering half of the city, we reached our destination. The place wasn't impressive in a happy sort of way, but at a glance, I got the feeling that this place had a lot to talk about and that was something that would make Mr.Beckham happy. We parked our bikes at random places and then settled down at the shade of a long, branched, ancient looking tree in the far right corner of the church. The church was ruined, that was clear but it stood in might, even past so many centuries, its walls dark grey with intricate patterns and drawings all over it, which was clearly a time consuming work and also the evidence of a great artist.

"So, nice choice anyway." said Aiden, looking around.

"Where do we start?" Layla asked. "I know a bit about the history…or let's say myths about this place. My grandmother used to say those stories to me before I slept."

"What myth?" I asked her, feeling the curiousness rise in me.

"I don't know if it's true but more than a hundred years ago, this place, as I said earlier, was used for devil or demonic worship. It was a time when religion or faith, was considered a really important part of one's life, so there was chaos everywhere as no one knew who was a friend or foe." She said. I got the feeling of sitting in a history classroom but a more interesting one and it was pretty clear that Layla had an eye for stuff like this.

"Why not? Why was it difficult to understand between friend and foe?" asked Muriel, balancing her elbows on her knees and leaning forward.

"Well at that time no one revealed who they were worshipping- God or Satan. People who seemed like believers in God might not actually be a believer." Layla explained. "But one day, people who supported God came out with a plan. They decided to sneak into the place at night and find out who all were there. It was hard to find people who agreed to come, so there were only a handful of them. On a Friday night, they came here but were shocked to find almost 15-20 people lying there on the floor, dead. They were all covered in black robes and it was clear from their clothing that some kind of ceremony had been going on. But till now, no one has been able to provide a practical or a proper solution to how so many people could have died, with no signs of violence and not even a sound escaping. As people feared that this would rise again, they blew the place to bits, but even then, as you can see, it survived. People later called it a miracle evidence, the defeat of good over evil."

"That's one hell of a bedtime story." Aiden whispered.

If what she said was true, then we were sitting right now at a place where twenty people had mysteriously died and that thought alone was enough to send a shiver down my spine. I wanted to run but I didn't.

"Are we allowed to go inside?" asked Muriel.

"Are you human?! Layla just said that people died here." Aiden said, looking flustered.

"Yeah well, I heard it and I don't buy it but still I would like to go inside and check out the place." she said.

"We came here to do the assignment. So let's get that done first and then we can hang around this place." Layla suggested. That was agreed upon; we divided the topics among us and set to work. I got the architecture and Layla got myths (of course), Muriel got the location and its importance while Evan and Aiden worked on the history. Even though we tried paying attention to the work we were doing, it was clear that we were all distracted. Aiden got startled every few seconds and Muriel did not lose a chance to tease him, cracking up all of us. It was different to be around new people and for the first time I hoped that I had made some friends before. Seeing clearly that we were not getting anywhere with the assignment, we decided to walk around the place. We walked carefully, trying not to disturb things or according to Muriel 'rise the spirits of the dead', our small voices echoing through the pillars and stones. I felt the designs and shapes under my palm as I ran my hand across the walls and pillars that had sustained the attack. I was so lost in thought that I practically jumped when Evan tripped over and fell. We all ran to his side but he seemed fine and was already on his feet, when Layla exclaimed. "Hey look at this." She said, holding up a bottle. "This is what Evan tripped over."

"Isn't it a piece of the pillar?" asked Evan, moving closer. "It has all those designs on it."

"No... I don't think so, look carefully." She said. We moved in closer to get a good look but saw no difference. Seeing our puzzled looks, Layla shook her head and said, "Do you see the figures on the jar? That shows people worshipping God, so it means that it is done in an ethical religious way. Whereas, when you look at the walls, you see circular patterns, which shows that the work is in Bohemian style."

"Wow, you know a lot." Evan said, looking impressed.

I moved over to the walls and saw that she was right. "So what do you think that is then?" I asked.

"It looks like a bottle. Maybe we should open it and see if there's anything inside." Muriel said. Layla twisted open the top but as soon as she did it, the slight breeze turned into a strong wind, pulling at our hairs, darkening the sky above and just like it started, it ended too.

"What was that?" asked Aiden, looking clearly worried.

"You call that a strong wind, Aiden." Muriel said, snickering. "It's turning dark, let's go."

"Well, it didn't feel like a usual "strong wind"… "Aiden said and Evan and I exchanged a smile.

*****

I looked at the red carpets before me, leading all the way towards the entrance of the art show and then around me, to make sure no one was watching. It was around seven in the evening and I had called Morgan to see if she was still here. Brianna had left early but she stayed for some time more and so I decided to drop by. Seeing no one around, I walked through the red carpets in all style, waving back at the invisible people, who were all excitedly waving at the famous Samuel Colton. I smiled to myself and walked into the cool air of the building, hoping beyond hope that no one had seen it. I met Morgan after a few exhibits, staring at a painting, her chin held up as if balanced on something invisible. "What's that about?"

She turned around and smiled at me. "Illuminati, I think. The owl was one of their signs."

The painting was the magnified version of the eye of an owl, inside it people were standing around doing rituals and sacrifices. It was beautifully drawn and nicely conveyed. "Nice."

"It's weird isn't? That people are always trying to find an answer to this so called power?" she said, her eyes still lingering on the painting.

"Have you? Found the answer?"

She smiled. "No one in history ever has Sam. That is why it's so hard for me to believe it."

She left half an hour later, leaving me between thoughts of my mind and strokes of many an unknown brush.

CHAPTER THREE

It was around eight when I finished an entire round of the show, staring at the painting, giving it my own interpretations and then reading the inscriptions below. On my way home, I found myself thinking about today morning and how I had enjoyed their company. At least I didn't want to run and hide in my room and that is definitely something. Layla and Evan had an argument on who would take the weird bottle home and they finally decided on Layla as she was so hysterical about it and started calling it the "Ancient Flagon".

As I drove through the night thinking about today, my ears picked up an unusual sound. I hit the brakes and stood there listening, trying to process what it was; a slow moaning. I looked around and found that I was near river

Fleei's south bank and it was so dark that I couldn't see anything clearly around me. I left the bike there and started walking towards the lake's bank, the sound becoming more distinct with every step I took, lights shimmering like dots on the opposite bank. It was turning windy and I pulled my hoodie over my head to stop the cold. As my eyes adjusted to the darkness, I saw someone sitting along the far end of the river. I couldn't make out whether it was a man or a woman but the long flowing hair made me guess it was a lady.

"Excuse me?... Is everything all right?" I asked her. She tilted her head a little but did not reply. She seemed to be washing something. Some cloth. Even though I just wanted to turn around and go, I walked closer towards her, wanting to find out if she was alright.

"I was riding my bike close by and I heard a sound. Are you all right? Do you…" I stopped midway noticing what she was washing. The cloth looked oddly familiar but that's not what caught my attention. It was the deep red patches she was washing from it.

"Is that…is that blood?!" I asked. She tilted her head again but did not reply.

"Are you all right? Do you want some help…I…I can help you"

Then she turned and as if on cue, my blood froze. A sweat broke down in my lower back as my brain tried hard to believe what my eyes saw. She looked like an animal, small but ugly. Her swollen eyes travelled all the way, looking at me, from head to toe and I felt as though I was being scanned and like a stimuli, the heat rose in my cheeks. Her nostrils were big but disproportionate. Her feet looked like that of a duck, like it was webbed. She had long hanging breasts that almost touched her knees. She stared at me with those animal-like eyes and all I wanted to do was run but I stood there, my feet glued to the ground, not knowing what to do. Then all of a sudden, she started walking towards me, swinging the cloth in a wide arc. All the impulses in my body screamed in panic and I ran. I ran as fast as I could, jumped onto my bike and drove away. I did not look back until I reached my house and I stood at the porch listening to the sounds of my shallow breath. I went into the house checking each room to see if everyone was safe. Finding everyone in their beds, I went to my bedroom and lay on the bed, not bothering to change into my pajamas. The lady's face came back to my mind, as though imprinted behind my eyelids. I went back and forth in those memories trying to find something that made sense, anything to prove me wrong. I never hoped to sleep that night but I was proved wrong as the day's exhaustion waved through me.

The night was more exhausting than the day; the dreams clear and scary. I sat up in bed and felt my leg muscles hurt, probably the running and pedaling from last night. I pushed the thoughts of last night out of my mind and got up to get dressed. I ran down the stairs and stuffed my breakfast quickly into my mouth as my sister stared at me.

"Clearly, you are not hungry, Sam." She said with her usual tint of sarcasm.

"Shut up Brianna!" I grabbed my bag and ran out of the door, shouting goodbyes. I rode quickly towards the river Fleei and stopped by its side, adamant to find something that would prove me wrong. There wasn't anything I expected to see, except filthy garbage dumped here and there. (I hated how no one seemed to care about the planet).There was no sign of the weird lady or any blood stained dress. I looked around for some more time but as I was late for school, I left, riding as fast as I could and sliding stop in front of Morgan.

"Ohh…finally, Sam! Where the hell have you been? Do you know what the time is?" she looked troubled and there were dark circles under her eye that said that she had not slept well. I started apologizing to her as we walked through the rush people.

"Sam, I need to talk to you. It's … It's something important." She looked like she had had a very long night. I was going to ask what was wrong but then I stopped talking. My breath narrowed and my hands shook as I stared at what she was wearing.

"Morgan…this dress…where?" my voice was barely a whisper. She wore a white dress that hung lazily around her body, ending just above her knees. I had seen her in this dress before. But I had seen it - last night. With blood stains. With that weird, old lady. Her expression changed as she studied me and I was pretty sure that I looked as pale as the moon.

"Hey, are you all right?" she shook me by my shoulder. "Why did you ask about the dress?" she sounded troubled which was unusual. The bell rang and I shuddered, waking me up from my stunned form. I let out a deep breath and smiled. "Morgan, I will meet you at the cafeteria during lunch. You can tell me what you wanted to say." Seeing her expression I said, "Morgan… I am all right. I'll see you." With that I walked away, my mind in a swirl of thoughts and emotions, fear dominating all.

*****

Even though I was physically in class, my mind roamed around various things. I was not sure whether it was Morgan's dress I had seen in the lady's hands. Surely there could be more of those dresses. And even if it was Morgan's, if the lady had to take it, Morgan would have seen her. Is that what she wanted to tell me? As the bell rang for lunch, I grabbed my bag and ran as fast as I could towards the cafeteria. I sat at our usual spot waiting for her to come, my finger beating on the table with impatience.

"Hey Samuel, over here" I turned around to see Aiden and Layla waving at me, the pink haired girl beside her. I waved back and then pointed at Morgan who was coming towards me. They flashed a thumbs up and I smiled and turned to face Morgan. I could make out one thing from her face, she was far from fine. Her bright eyes lacked their shine and her posture showed clear signs of exhaustion.

"Morgan, what is it that you wanted to tell?" I asked.

She spoke in a low tone. "I don't know. It might sound crazy to you. But……"

"Morgan, it's me and I will believe you." I stretched my hand and took hers in mine. She sighed and then spoke. "Yesterday night I was not able to sleep. Actually I was sleeping, but I woke up in the middle of the night and I felt like I couldn't breathe, like someone was strangling me. I wanted to cry for help but I couldn't find my voice. And then…" she rubbed her stomach with her free hand.

So let's be frank, I was a bit disappointed that she was not here to talk about that weird lady. But then, I saw a tear trace her pink cheeks and I pressed her hand, reassuringly. She took a deep breath and continued. "Then I saw something sitting on top of me. It was … I don't know. It looked like a small bear or something. I wanted to push it away from me but I couldn't move my limbs... I … I felt like I was paralyzed or something." She looked like she might break down any minute. I did not know what to say. I wanted to tell her about the weird old lady but she looked like she had enough to deal with. There was silence for a long time.

"Morgan…it might have been a dream or something." I said, the only rational explanation that came to my mind and I felt a twinge of disappointment wave through me as I said it, as if I wasn't giving it my everything. She fixed me with a long stare and I had known her long enough to know that she had been expecting this reply from me. Just then the school bell rang. Breaking her stare, she got up, swinging her bag onto her shoulders.

"My dad is going to pick me up today. I am too tired to ride. So see you tomorrow then." She hugged me and walked away. My eyes followed her all the way until she was out of sight. I wanted to say something, to console her, to support her but I couldn't do it. I walked back to class, where I spent the entire day spiraling in my own maze and then headed home. With each step I took that day, I felt a small but dangerous fear rising in me as I thought about Morgan and everything she told me. I went home finding it empty and headed straight to my room, intending to get some sleep. I did not have to try hard because as soon as I hit the pillows, I blacked out.

*****

"Sam, wake up." My eyes fluttered and slowly came into vision. Brianna was standing there near me. I looked at the window and found that the sky had darkened.

"Sorry I overslept." I said, rubbing my eyes. She did not say anything. That was unusual; she always has something to say. I looked up and found that her eyes were puffed from crying.

"Brianna, what's wrong?" she looked at me but said nothing. I did not want to think what had gone wrong. "Speak up girl. What is wrong?!"

She spoke in a low voice "It's… It's Morgan."

CHAPTER FOUR

I ran. I ran as fast as I could towards Morgan's house. My legs begged me to stop and my lung told me to breathe, but, right now all that mattered was her. I did not stop until I reached her house. There were people everywhere. I ran towards the front door pushing people out of my path. I was not ready to believe that it had happened, but I knew deep down, that Brianna had told the truth. As I stood there at her front door, I knew that one of the most important people of my life had gone and the truth slapped me in the face. A million emotions waved through me. I felt grief beyond measure, I felt anger surge through me, I felt fear gripping me and above all I could taste the guilt that danced in my mouth.

A hand touched my shoulder and I turned around to find Brianna standing near me. She had regained control of herself, something I was completely incapable of. My tears traced down my cheeks all the way to the chin where they hung aimlessly. I tried to find my voice, I needed so many answers.

"How..?" I asked. If I hadn't known I was going to speak, I wouldn't have recognized the sound. My voice was hoarse and strained.

"It was some kind of lung damage. She slept after returning from school but ..." Brianna's voice broke. She couldn't finish what she was saying. But I knew she meant to say that she never woke up again. She took a deep breath and continued. "We have a funeral in two days, they are waiting for some relatives to arrive and I guess there are some formalities in the hospital too. I heard a few people around here speak of it."

I nodded because I did not know what else to do or say. I noticed her father sitting rigid and pale while her mother sat near him, tears running down their faces silently. Her father looked up at me and nodded as if he had lost all capability of speech. For what felt like forever, we stood there in the middle of the silent chaos, both of us not knowing what to do. Finally, I spoke up.

"Let's go home, it's suffocating here."

*****

"Let us pray that this little angel may rest in peace and let her family have the strength to overcome this loss. Amen."

"Amen" everyone said together.

I tried to say it, but I am not sure any voice came out. It had taken a while for this reality to sink in, but it did not necessarily mean that I had accepted it and I was not sure I wanted to. People slowly left, one by one, like water trickling down a tap. Her mother hugged me before she left, her father just nodded, and none of them spoke a word.

"I can't imagine what they are going through." Brianna held my hand as she spoke. I could see that she was trying her best to keep herself together.

"It's unfair." I said. Maybe that was the very first thing I said today and she nodded in agreement. We had become close these past two days. I had never really recognized how much she had grown up; there was so much of my mother's features in her, from her caring touch to the silent companionship. I was happy to have her with me, despite everything.

"Let's head home, it's becoming dark." She said, staring at the sky. I looked at the grave one more time and then walked away. The sky was dark and black, the clouds hiding the earth from whatever light it could get and we walked, side by side, in silence. On our way, we passed the Miles' manor. The house and its neighboring one were filled with people and by judging from their faces, they were not having a happy time.

"What's wrong?" I asked, pointing at the house.

"Oh, I heard that old Mr.Grant passed away last night. Not a good time for anyone, I guess." She shrugged. Mr.Grant lived near Evan and I used to see him when I was small, watering the plants in his garden or bathing his dogs. I thought about how Mr.Grant's family might be feeling; probably the same way Morgan's parents or I felt. But I was sure that none of them would ever feel the guilt or the hatred I had for myself for not believing what Morgan had said, making me think again if it was all interconnected. I looked away from the Grant house and continued walking, yet again in silence. The best thing about Brianna is that she never asked questions. She remained quiet all the way back home and I made a mental note to thank her later for this. When we reached home, mom and dad were discussing something, which they stopped as soon as they spotted us, making it pretty evident that it was about us, or rather, me.

"Hey Sam" my mom greeted me. I went and sat near her as Brianna spread herself in the arm chair.

"Sam, we know that Morgan's death affected you pretty badly…"

"Yeah dad, we can see that" Brianna intervened.

"But you should return to school, boy." he continued without paying her any attention. "You can't skip school, this is an important phase…but take your own time."

Till then the thought of going back to school had not occurred to me and it brought a lump in my throat. I couldn't possibly go back to school where her presence was felt so much. I looked at my parents and was sure they were expecting me to say something, so I spoke up.

"I will go back dad, that's for sure, but I need some time. Please." My parents did not look convinced, so I looked at Brianna for help.

"He needs a break. It's necessary. He will go back once things are sorted out. Right now, he needs some rest." With that she dragged me by the hand to my bedroom and told me to get some sleep. Well, it's easily said than done. Sleep was something I had grown a stranger to, in the past few days.

*****

Two weeks passed by. I sat at home, locked up in my bedroom; the only time I went out was when the house was empty. Evenings were the worst. I did not mind Brianna's company. She just sat with me and watched the show I was watching. She did not bother me with questions like how my day was or when I was planning to return to school, which, sadly, was the only thing my parents were interested in. Nights were filled with nightmares that made me wake up, bathed in sweat. No one asked me anything about how I felt and so I said nothing, letting the days go forward like this. And so on one such day, Brianna came to me.

"Hey." She said and sat down beside me. "We had a prayer meeting for the students who passed away."

"Students?" I raised my eyebrows.

"We had four deaths in our school the past two weeks, including Morgan." She said.

It shocked me to know that I had been completely oblivious of the outside world for so long now. "Oh God! Who else?" I wanted to know if it was someone I knew.

"Two guys and a girl. One is Allen Joyce, then a guy named Rease Skylar and a girl named Jocelyn Mateo." She studied me. "Do you know any of them?"

"I know Joyce. He was from my math class. He was a friend of Aiden." I said. "Aiden is a guy from my history assignment." I added. She looked at me for a while and then spoke up; "Sam, I am not forcing you to do anything, but just think about it. This girl who passed away, Mateo, her brother is in my class. He comes to school. He is quieter now and keeps mostly to himself, but at least he is trying to live his life. I am not saying to forget the past, but maybe loosen the grip on it by a bit. You need to give it a chance."

"Give what a chance?"

"Time, Sam. It heals people."

I did not know what to say and after a moment or two, we heard mom's muffled yell for dinner. Brianna sighed and went down. I was momentarily stuck and after a lot of internal discussion and debate, I headed down for dinner. The smell of roasted chicken filled my nostrils as I descended the steps, but the churning in my mind made my appetite vanish. I took a deep breath and sat down. Everyone was quiet for some time as we ate our food and I thought it was the best opportunity to speak up.

"Dad, mom, I am heading to school tomorrow."

To be honest I thought they would drop their spoons in shock and appreciate me for my decision. But all they did was shake their head at me in agreement and I am pretty sure that if anyone was surprised, it was me. After dinner, I went to my favorite place in the house, the indoor garden. I loved sitting among plants so it was basically my idea to have it, which is kind of a stupid one since we already have a garden. But gardens made me feel exposed and so I spent most of my time here. I had furnished it with a swing so that I could go out there sometimes to clear my head but never in my dreams had I imagined that my head would be such a mess. But sitting there, swinging to and fro in the moonlight, I felt more relaxed than I had been in these past two weeks. I stared at the only star in the sky that kept twinkling at me and wondered if it was Morgan and whether she was smiling at me. I stared at the star with such intensity that I was literally shocked when Brianna's voice filled the room.

"You never listen to me. What happened now?" I turned around and found her walking towards me. Her blue eyes glinted in the moonlight and she looked so much like me that the resemblance was kind of startling.

"Well, some situations can make you desperate enough to listen to your sister" I said. She laughed and so did I. Maybe Brianna was right, time heals.

CHAPTER FIVE

Being the center of attraction was something not at all attractive for an introvert like me. I was famous in school as Morgan's boyfriend and I was always with her. But today as I waked alone in the hallways at school, being the receiver of stares and hushed whispers, I understood that returning without her was the worst thing that could happen to me. I found out that her locker had been decorated by some students and I was pretty sure that if she had been here, she would have hated it. I looked around me in the hope of finding someone I knew, because for the first time in my life, I wanted not to be alone. My eyes wandered the hallways and stopped when they spotted Muriel Payton. As I got closer towards her, I found out that she was staring at another decorated locker. There was a picture of a handsome lean guy, with ruffled brown-black hair and shining eyes, in the front.

"Rease Skylar." I read. Muriel turned to face me.

"Hi Samuel"; she said in a low voice. She did not seem like her usual self.

"Sam" I said.

Her bushy black hair was tied up in a tight ponytail and I could see dark circles through her spectacles. She seemed to have lost some sleep.

"You knew him?" I asked.

"Yes, he was my…friend. We shared a few classes." She pursed her lips as if it was the end of the conversation. From the way she talked, I knew there was something more, but I did not press the subject.

"How are you holding up?" she asked.

"I am fine, I guess." I wished that was the truth.

"We should head to class. We have history together." She said. I was glad to have someone beside me but I knew from the looks of it that Muriel had had a difficult time too. She somehow changed. We chose a seat near the window in the classroom, at the far corner, away from people. I thought she might go sit with some of her friends but she sat with me and I did not mind having company. I saw Aiden sitting in front of me, his cap pulled over his face, the seat beside him empty. I wondered how Allen's death had affected him. As far as I had known, they were both very close. As Mr.Beckam was out of town, Mr.Anderson came to class. He said that Mr.Beckam would return in two days, which meant that we had the next forty-eight hours to finish our assignment. Evan, who sat behind me, poked me with his pen.

"Should we meet today to finish up?" he asked. He looked paler and thinner than the last time I had seen him.

"Yeah, okay. What about you, Muriel?" I asked.

"Sorry, what?" she asked as if she had woken up from a trance. Evan let out a growl like he was irritated so I repeated what he had said.

"I am in." she said. "What about the other two?"

"Let's check with them at lunch." I said. Evan nodded and slid back in his seat.

*****

Layla, Evan, Muriel, Aiden and I rode our way to the churchyard. It wasn't as cheerful and pleasant as it had been the last time we had gathered. From what Muriel said, Layla had lost her best friend, Jocelyn Mateo, the girl with the pink hair and that hit her pretty hard. Evan was also close to his neighbor in the Grant house. It seemed like each one of us had had a bad time. We sat down in the same place as last time and started our work. We finished pretty quickly as most of us were silent, the atmosphere around us devoid of laughter and fun. As we packed our bags to leave, Layla removed a bottle from her bag and placed it at her feet.

"Wait" I said; "Isn't that…what did you call it?"

"Ancient flagon"; Aiden provided.

"Yeah. Ancient flagon." I said. "Are you trying to get rid of it?"

"Yes". She said. "I guess it brings bad luck." She added hesitantly.

"Oh please! Bad luck from a bottle?" Muriel shook her head like this idea was outrageous.

"You don't understand" she said as a tear slid down her cheek.

"Yeah, I seriously don't understand how you can be so superstitions." Muriel said.

And then Layla shouted, which was kind of unusual for a quiet and withdrawn girl like her. "What do you want me to do then?! Two days after I take this bottle home, I find this scary lady washing blood off my best friend's dress. The next day Jocelyn wears the same dress to school and says that she suffered from sleep paralysis. And then before I could even think about it, I hear that she died. Do you think that all of this is a complete coincidence?"

Layla turned pale from shouting. But she wasn't the only one. Aiden, Muriel and Evan turned pale as well and from the way my hands were shaking, I am pretty sure that I turned pale too. There was a very long moment of silence. My stomach did a somersault as I realized that Layla had seen what I had seen. My mouth went dry and I am sure that I would have thrown up if Evan hadn't spoken.

"You saw that lady too?"

PART TWO

"It's so much darker when a light goes out,
than it would have been if it had never shone."
— John Steinbeck,
The Winter of our Discontent.

CHAPTER SIX

"Layla, what actually is this sleep paralysis?" Aiden asked. We had gathered under the tree again to discuss.

"Well, after Jocelyn told me about what happened…" she began, "…I went home and researched. From what I read, I understood that sleep paralysis was actually a part of a dream. There are scientific explanations as well as a lot of myths and Jocelyn's story was more related to the myths. You feel breathlessness and your body becomes temporarily paralyzed. You lose your voice so you are unable to shout for help too. It matched exactly with what Jocelyn had said." She finished. Her brown hair played with the light breeze and her eyes were puffed red from crying. I felt like crying too because now I felt more miserable than ever for not believing what Morgan had said. I should have used my sense. Morgan had always been sensible and if she said something like this then it had to be true. Maybe, if I had believed Morgan, I could have helped her. The thought burned my insides.

"Everything suited from what Jocelyn had said." Layla continued. "Except one thing."

"What's that?" Evan asked.

"According to what I read from the myths" Layla started explaining, "people who experience sleep paralysis see a white faceless figure, almost human, sitting or lying on top of them. But what Jocelyn said was that she saw some furry bear-like creature sitting on her. That confused me."

"Morgan also said something about a bear." I added.

Evan said. "All that Mr.Grant said was that he felt paralyzed when he woke up in the middle of the night."

"Allen also mentioned it." Aiden confirmed.

"I am clueless. I have no idea about Rease." Muriel said. "I just saw the lady near the lake washing blood off a shirt. I found out it was his shirt only when he wore it the next day."

For a while we sat in silence, thinking. The sun had set and darkness started to creep through the churchyard. It was way past time to get home but all I wanted now was to sit with them. It seemed weird because I was sure that I felt more close to them than I have ever felt at home. Maybe home wasn't a place, after all.

"We should check near river Fleei" Muriel said.

"It's getting dark". Aiden said, looking around him.

"Have you heard of something called the flashlight, Aiden?" Evan asked. He rolled his eyes and Aiden shrugged.

"Evan, I think it's too late." I spoke up. "Our parents don't know where we are and if we be getting late anymore they are going to freak out, with all that's happening around here. And I don't think roaming around in the dark is safe either. We will go after school tomorrow."

"Sam has a point, Evan." Muriel said. Evan just shrugged as we started grabbing our bags and brushing dirt off our jeans.

"What about the ancient flagon?" Muriel asked.

Everyone seemed hesitant to take it.

"I will take it" I said. Well, what could possibly go wrong anymore?

"I don't think it's safe." Layla said. She looked disturbed.

"Well, let's see." I said and took the bottle from Muriel. The flagon was cold against my skin and I could feel a wretchedness. I pushed the thought out of my mind and tucked it in my bag.

*****

"SAMUEL COLTON, YOU ARE THE WORST BROTHER EVER!"; Brianna shut the door with so much force that my wardrobe nearby shook. She stormed into the room and threw a pillow at me. "Why the hell do you have a phone? You could have called me."

"You were tensed?" I asked, trying to hide my grin.

She shook her head; "You are despicable" she sighed and sat down.

"Dad and mom did not seem so tensed" I said, grinning

"So?" she sounded angry. "Where were you anyway?"

"Mmm…" I hesitated. "I was hanging out, alone, some quiet time."

She raised one eyebrow and then grinned. "You are a very pathetic liar. Do you know that?"

"I know it now. Thanks for enlightening me."

"You are welcome." She got up and left.

I had been afraid Brianna would ask me where I really was but she did not seem interested. I lay down in bed staring at the ceiling. These past two weeks had been a roller coaster ride but I had a hunch that things were going to get messier.

*****

"Eww… this clay is sticking onto my shoes." Muriel grumbled.

"Hmm I wonder why the clay would do that." Evan grinned.

We were near river Fleei now. It had been raining all day and the sand was wet and slippery. I could feel my heart pounding against my chest and I tried to hide my panic, probably like the rest of them.

"I don't think there is anyone here." Evan said, looking bored. We were walking so close that our shoulders hit against each other and I felt like he was speaking in my ear.

"You know what you signed up for, Evan." Muriel said, "We need to look deeper. You can't possibly expect the lady to come out and present herself to us."

"Yeah I don't think anyone would come out. They would be too freaked out by your ridiculous scarf." Evan snickered.

"This scarf is the closest thing I have to my mother." Muriel said turning around. She walked forward and I ran to catch up to her. "What happened to your mother?" I asked.

"Car accident. Didn't see that coming. Left my dad, my sibling and me alone." Muriel said.

"I am sorry." I said.

"Don't be." She said shaking her head. "I was just two years old when it happened. So I don't remember her much. This was hers." She said motioning towards the scarf.

"Can I ask you something Sam?" she asked, raising her eyebrows.

"Sure, anything." I said. She looked hesitant and I wondered what it could be.

"What was it like…you know" she asked, not meeting my eyes. It took me a few seconds to understand what she meant. I dug my hands deeper into my sweater pockets, not knowing what to say.

"It was difficult." I managed to say at last. "She was the only companion I had and suddenly she wasn't there anymore and it was…dreadful to cope with." Muriel did not say anything and for a brief moment it felt like I was walking with Brianna and not Muriel.

"You did not seem close to Skylar" I said. As soon as the words came out, I knew it had come out wrong. I was bad with words.

"I am sorry. That was not the right way to put it." I said. She smiled and I took in the fact that she looked beautiful when she smiled.

"It's okay Sam. It's just that… Rease had a strong… liking for me which I have been trying to avoid for a long time. We had an argument the day before he died. I was freaked out because of the shirt and I did not say that to him because I did not want him to think that I was being silly and superstitious."

"Which you clearly are not." I added. I had noticed that fact about her because Morgan was like that too.

She smiled again and continued; "So I was annoyed with him and we argued and I stormed out. That was the last I saw of him or talked to him. I couldn't even say sorry."

I looked at Muriel and thought about the grief she felt, the guilt of not having smoothed things over with Rease and the sadness that loomed over her because of this. Unknowingly, I found myself speaking, "Morgan told me everything, but I assured her it was just a bad dream. I knew she wouldn't make up something like that but I still didn't do anything. I had the power to right things, but I didn't."

"Some things can't be righted, Sam." Muriel said. I was going to reply when Layla spoke up.

"There is nothing here. We should find some other way to clear things up."

We stopped in our tracks and looked at each other. We had reached a dead end with not even a single clue to clarify our doubts. As if reading my mind, Aiden spoke up.

"What do we do now?" I thought this over for some time and then said, "If you guys don't mind we can go over to my house and discuss."

****

I never thought that bringing these guys home would be such a mess. Brianna opened the door, looking at me and then at them, her eyes demanding an explanation.

"These are my friends." I said.

"Your friends?

"We are doing a history assignment together."

"Your friends?" she repeated as if she couldn't believe it and I couldn't blame her. "... Hmm come in guys." She said, eyeing me curiously.

"Seems like your brother makes a lot of friends." Evan said, winking at Brianna. I pushed him up the stairs and rolled my eyes at my sister. Layla kept lurking behind, admiring the my father's collection of paintings and Aiden had to finally pull her along. We went to my indoor garden and settled down.

"Oh wow, I might need a place like this to come and calm my temper down… which means I might need it often." Evan said looking around.

"I have seen your sister before with Jocelyn's brother." Layla said. I knew Brianna had a lot of fans, but I didn't think she ever had a boyfriend, not to my knowledge anyway. So seeing the apparent look of surprise in my face she added quickly; "Not like that Sam, in his class. It is hard not to notice her."

"So, what exactly are we planning to do? Where do we start from?" Muriel asked, settling down on the floor.

"I don't know" I admitted, "Let's just go back and rewind the incident. There might be something we missed the first time."

"Will doing that be any good?" Aiden asked.

"We don't have a know-it-all person to give us some information, so this is the best we can do." I said.

"Which era are you guys living in?"

We all turned around to find Brianna standing in the doorway, leaning against the wall.

"Brianna please, go away" I said. The last thing I wanted was to involve my sister in this mess. She rolled her eyes and said, "If I wanted some information, I would look it up on the internet." Seeing no response, she shrugged and left. But the silence was not what she thought it was; it was pure, pure awe. Why hadn't it occurred to me before?

"Your sister is a genius." Muriel said, smiling her beautiful smile.

"It's not about being a genius; it's about having common sense." Aiden said matter-of-factly.

"Ok, brain of the operation" Muriel retorted.

"But about what do we search exactly?" asked Evan.

"About the lady" I said. "We will keep adding descriptions and everything we saw until we get a hint." Even though no one said anything, I knew that they all had agreed.

I borrowed Brianna's laptop, which she gave with a smirk. She knew her point had helped. I took my laptop, gave Brianna's to Evan and the rest of them bent down on their phones.

"Does your sister have a boyfriend?" asked Evan.

"Uhhh…not to my knowledge." I said, awkwardly. He gave me a thumbs up, I had no idea for what, and got to work.

The following one hour was filled with beeps from phones and small murmurs. After a tiring hour, everyone had given up except Evan. An idea which seemed like a good one now seemed ridiculous.

"Give up Evan", said Muriel leaning against the wall.

"No way, girl. My conscience won't let me admit defeat". He said shaking his head. I leaned against the bed-post and thought whether this firm decision had anything to do with it being Brianna's idea.

"I told you I would make it!" said Evan, half an hour later, banging his arm on a pillow. "Come over here, people."

We all gathered around him on the bed and looked into the screen. As our eyes took in the picture, we all gasped at the same instant. There she was, looking at us through her glassy eyes. Even though the picture looked different here and there, it was her anyway. We had found her. My eyes moved towards the top of the page and read the heading, "Bean nighe?"

CHAPTER SEVEN

"A Bean Nighe is a Scottish mythical creature", read Aiden "This creature is believed to be a messenger like Hermes."

"Who is Hermes?" asked Evan.

"He is a Greek god. He was the messenger of the greater Greek gods like Zeus." Aiden said.

"Damn. How do you know all those?" asked Muriel.

"Big brain." Aiden said, smiling.

"Who's Zeus?" asked Evan again.

"It doesn't matter. Aiden, please continue." Layla said impatiently.

Aiden cleared his throat and continued; "According to the stories, she is not harmful but she is considered a bad omen as she is associated with death." He swallowed and read; "In the stories, the bean nighe can be found washing blood off the dress belonging to the person whose death is near. Even though she doesn't mean any harm, it is believed that she can break a person's bone with the cloth that she possesses".

Aiden stopped reading and we all sat in silence. Some things were settled now. We had all seen the bean nighe. She was the messenger of death and she could break bones with a cloth. Interesting. But she was a mythical creature, so she couldn't be real. How then had we seen her? My swirl of thoughts were disturbed when Muriel's phone rang and she went out into the balcony to pick it up.

"It's my dad" she said, coming back. "I need to get to home now. He was worried sick."

"We all should" said Aiden. "We will meet tomorrow here, if that is ok." I nodded.

They grabbed their bags and headed out of the room. Evan held Brianna's laptop and started going down the stairs. At the bottom he met Brianna and handed it to her. "Thank you, Brianna. Your idea helped us" he said. "By the way, I am Evan Miles."

I turned around smiling, now being sure about why he was so interested to find the clue. I couldn't blame him, my sister had quite an effect on people.

"See you guys then." I said waving. Muriel turned towards me part way across the lawn. She opened her mouth to say something, but only waved and headed out. I stood there for a moment and then I ran towards her.

"Muriel, what is it?" I asked. She hesitated for a bit.

"I need to tell you something. It's just a hunch but I wanted you to know first before I tell the others." She said glancing back at their figures moving into the night.

"And that is…?" I asked. She turned and spoke. "Grab your keys."

*****

"Muriel, where are we going?" We were very far away from my house now. We had stopped at her house to tell her dad that she wanted to go to school to grab a book she forgot and since then, it had been almost five minutes of continuous driving. My legs ached as I tried to catch up with her. 'God, she is fast.' I thought.

"For heaven's sake!" I stopped my bike to catch my breath. She turned around and headed back towards me.

"Sam, it's getting late, we need to get there before my dad calls to check in on me."

"Get where?" I asked through deep breaths.

"It's around that corner." She said pointing at a road that turned right just a few feet away. "Okay, listen to me now. I was riding back the other day from school…before we went to the church to complete the assignment… I had taken the long way back home and saw Reese's older brother, Ryan. He stopped to talk to me and I asked him what he was doing out here. He said that he had come to attend a funeral of a distant relative. When I asked him what had happened, he said that the death had occurred when the guy was asleep. It did not sound weird to me then, but now after all that we have discussed and read…this seems unusual." She said all of it at once that she had to stop and catch her breath before she spoke again. I looked into her eyes, trying to understand her.

"What do you think?"

"I don't know." And that was the truth. I did not know what to make out of what she had said. "Muriel, this could have been a coincidence. Maybe we are overthinking things." I could see the triumph in her eyes vanish as soon as I said it.

"Are we going to the house of the guy who died?" I asked her.

"Yeah, we were. We are heading back now." With that she rode her bicycle in the opposite direction. I peddled as fast as possible to catch up with her.

"Muriel, see it's…" I began, but she interrupted.

"It was just a hunch." She said and pursed her lips in the same manner she did earlier. We rode the rest of the way back in silence. I understood that I had somehow broken a bond in a very, very stupid way and kept wondering how I could mend it. I could have just gone with her and maybe she could have been right. I had guessed that she felt open with me after the small talk we had near the lake, but after this I doubted if it would be the same anymore. I was so much absorbed in my thoughts that I did not realize that we had reached her house until she called out. I kicked the brakes, the machine straining against the sudden action.

"Goodnight. I will see you tomorrow." Muriel said and without meeting my eyes, walked towards her house. I stood there, looking at her walk into the darkness, her mom's scarf a whirl of red in the black. Halfway across, she turned and headed back towards me.

"Sam…I chose to tell you because I thought that you might believe even the wildest theories after what you have been through…you know, even after not being able to do anything about Morgan. That's why I chose to tell you first. But maybe you are right, maybe we are overthinking things." "Goodnight" she added after a beat. She hesitated for a while, then walked across the garden to her house. She did not turn back to look at me this time because if she had she would have spotted the tears that ran down my face. I mounted my bike and rode back home. My tears did not stop and I made no attempt to do so. What Muriel had said was true. I should have believed her. I hated her for looking at me in the face and telling me that I did nothing to stop my girlfriend's death. But more than that, I felt that she did me a great favor, that somehow she helped me believe the truth and for the first time in many days I cried like it was the end of the world. I stopped my bike and slid out of it, my sobs filling the silent night. I sat on the moist floor, not even caring about the mud that stuck to my clothes and sobbed into my hands. I was alone and nothing in this whole wide world could reverse my actions.

"Are you all right?"

I jerked up on my legs, ready to hit whoever it was, but instead my eyes met another pair of green ones, the pupils dilated in fear. A young boy, smaller than me, was standing there looking as afraid and scared as I was.

"I just wanted to help…I am sorry" he said.

"It's alright. Hi, I am Samuel. What are you doing out here?" I asked and that is when I really looked around. I was near river Fleei.

"Hi, I am Mathew." The boy introduced.

"WHAT ARE YOU DOING OUT HERE?!" I asked him again but this time I literally screamed in the boy's face. Seeing the panic in his eyes I said more calmly, "Mathew, right? OK see it is not very safe out here. You should get home."

"But I want to look around." He said.

"Why don't you do that tomorrow morning?" I suggested.

He remained silent for a while as if he was thinking, then shook his head. "I did that already but it's no use."

"Mathew, come back in the morning, whatever it is, you will find it much quicker in daylight." I pleaded.

"No I won't find her if I come in the morning." He said in a low voice.

"Find who?" I asked. I could feel my heart pacing and my tears sticking onto my face. What had this boy seen?

"That…lady" Mathew said.

CHAPTER EIGHT

"Impossible! It might be someone else, ok? How can… that's not…HOW?!"

"Calm down Aiden. Let Sam finish." Evan said, motioning me to continue. We were all sitting around my room again, as we had planned yesterday.

"Mathew said that he saw a big scary lady near river Fleei on a day when he was returning home late, after a match. He said he saw her wash something red from his mother's dress and he freaked out when he saw her, so he ran away. He told me that the bean nighe had not seen him, but we can't be sure of that." I finished.

"This might have no particular connection with what you just said, but can I ask you *why* you were near the river, at that time, even though you know that it can be dangerous?" Layla asked, looking at me, doubtfully.

"And Layla, just like you said, it doesn't matter, does it? So, let's just work things out right now." Muriel said, scrolling through her phone, not meeting my eyes. Since morning, I seemed pretty invisible to her. I knew that she was saving me the embarrassment but I didn't want that. I trusted these people and right now the best thing to do would be to speak the truth.

"We went somewhere last night." I began.

"We?" asked Aiden.

"Muriel and I. She had a hunch and she asked me to go with her. I went but I just waved her doubts away saying that she was overthinking. But at the end, she was right."

"Why didn't you include us? We didn't seem as trustworthy as him?" asked Evan, looking thoroughly displeased about it.

"Thanks, you made things so much better for me." Muriel said, giving me a deadly glance.

"Hey, I don't think she did anything wrong." Layla spoke up. "See, it was better that she didn't take us. Maybe it was for our own safety and we don't have to get upset about it." A lame excuse, really, but I was grateful for it. "But I guess we should make sure we don't do that again, that whatever happens, we tell each other. Even though we only know each other, for like…a few weeks, I think that we have been through a lot together."

"We can start calling ourselves a *gang*" said Aiden, smiling.

"No one calls anyone a *gang* anymore, Aiden." Evan smiled and I saw that each one of us were smiling at each other. What Layla said was true, we might have known other people for a longer time but what we had right now was far stronger than anything that could bind people; secrets.

"She's right. We have faced fear together, now we fight fear together too. That's something that binds us. Something that defines our friendship." I said, looking out of the window. There was silence for some time so I looked around to find them all staring at me and the color rose in my cheeks immediately.

"I have a doubt" said Evan, "How exactly are you related to Shakespeare?"

And we all burst out laughing, the tension in the air slowly melting away. The time was so good that I wanted to freeze it then and there, nothing about the past or nothing about the future worried me, all that mattered was me and my friends. 'Friends', the word echoed in my head.

"Hmm, on a more serious note, if Mathew saw what he saw, then that means that his mother is in danger and we are the only ones who know that, right?" Evan asked. "What do we do?"

"We should go over to his house and maybe look around a bit, this might be our only chance to save the lady as well as get a clue on what that thing is." said Aiden in his matter-of-fact voice. We all agreed and slowly started moving out of the room. I was grabbing a few random stuff that I figured might be of use, when a voice spoke behind me.

"Hey", I turned around to find Muriel standing near me. "So, you *can* see me." I replied.

"Look Sam, I am so sorry that I was mean to you yesterday and I didn't mean what I said. You are not responsible for Morgan's death in any way and I am sorry I said that."

"You don't have to be sorry about it. In fact, what you said…was true. I could have helped her. And I didn't, so maybe I did have a role in it. 'The darkest places of hell are reserved for those who remain silent.'" I said, looking at her.

"Dan Brown, huh?" she replied. I was surprised that she knew it and I pointed at the book shelf as an answer.

She looked like she wanted to say something but nothing came out of her. And then out of the blue, she hugged me.

"I am sorry that you had to lose her. And I don't think you have a role in it, even if you think so." Her voice was barely a whisper and I couldn't have heard her if she was not so near. "I know that nothing you do can bring her back, but you can save a lot of people from this. She gave you a head start, to save the people that lived in the same place she called home." She slowly pulled away. "Don't let her down because if you do, that would actually play a role in destroying her memory."

I nodded my head not knowing what to say. After a second, I said, "So how exactly are *you* related to Shakespeare?" She laughed her beautiful laugh and we both headed downstairs, my mind happy that I had made up for what I did last night, that I had mended something that I unknowingly broke. I knew that all five of them made me feel something, something I never experienced before- the warmth of friendship. I felt it in their smiles, I felt it in Muriel's hug, I felt it around me. For the first time in many years, I prayed that I never lose these people.

*****

An hour later we gathered around Mathew's house, standing on the pathway opposite it, not knowing what to do. It was a simple and beautiful little house, with creepers hanging down its walls. We decided to look around without evoking suspicion. Layla, Evan, and I went around one side and Muriel and Aiden went around the other. We peaked in through a window to find a lady, in her thirties, sitting on a spread chair, reading the newspaper. She looked a lot like Mathew, with his eyes and lean physique, so she must be his mother and we assumed that she is safe, at least for now. This also meant that there was a good chance of catching sight of whatever might take place. We walked back and caught up with the other two.

"Even if we see it, whatever 'it' is, what are we going to do?" asked Layla, sitting down in a bench around the corner. We all fell silent as we thought about the question. She was right; we had no idea what to do. Needless to say, we did not even know what might show up.

"We need a plan and a good one too." said Muriel. "I have one in mind but it doesn't make much sense. Phase one would be to wait, find some place nearby that would not attract much attention so as to avoid looking like creeps. That would be a bit difficult with Evan around."

"Hey." Evan protested while the rest of us sniggered.

"Phase two would be to encounter it. We need to be equipped for that."

"Equipped with what?" asked Aiden. "How do we equip ourselves without knowing what we are going to face? That's totally ridiculous."

"What other choice do we have other than getting killed? We must be prepared, have things in general, say like, something you can hit with." suggested Evan.

"It seems pretty good to me. This is all we can do right now with what little information we have." I spoke up, even though the hitting part seemed a bit far-fetched. "Few of us should go get things for protection while the rest find a place to settle down." We discussed and decided that Aiden and Evan will go in search for whatever they can find, while Muriel, Layla and I stayed back and tried to find a place close by. We walked around the lane for a while, looking for an appropriate place to stay and keep watch. Finally, after a few rounds around the place we found an abandoned building, a place which was under construction but for some reason left unfinished. Muriel texted Evan to let them know that where we were and also to bring a binocular, then climbed up the building.

The floorboards creaked under our feet as we climbed, dust rising in puffs of smoke near our legs. We found a cleaner space on the third floor, which gave almost a good view of Mathew's house. We spread a sheet Layla had brought and settled down on it.

"Is it just me or do you all feel unnaturally calm?" asked Muriel, her eyes fixed at some far unknown place.

"It's not just you. It is scientifically proven that if you are close to something you don't want to face but still have to, then you face the situation calmly. It's in human nature." Layla said. I looked at the city that sprawled under us. It looked small and beautiful, people happy and contented, sitting relaxed at their houses not knowing that probably something bad was about to happen, letting a few seventeen-year-olds handle the issues that bothered the place. After what Muriel said, I loved this city more. This green and small place is the place that Morgan called home, the place I call home, the place my friends call home and I knew at once that I needed to protect it, no matter what. After half an hour or so, we heard footsteps approaching and looked around to find Evan and Aiden walk over to us. They showed us the things they gathered- a baseball bat (a baseball bat?), some flashlights, some blankets and some binoculars. We surveyed the things they had brought and then sat around in a circle, Evan and Aiden at my sides.

"And we brought you guys something else. Surprise!" Evan grabbed a package of sandwiches from his bag.

"Knew you guys were hungry, so Uncle Evan bought you people, lovely Brim's sandwiches."

We ate in silence, taking turns to look at the house to see if things were all right. It was late afternoon and I texted Brianna to tell her that I might be late to reach home. "Dude, why do you keep smelling like dog food?" asked Muriel, taking a whiff and crinkling her eyebrows at Evan.

"I spend almost all of my time with dogs, I love them more than humans, well with a few exceptions." He said looking at all of us. "That's why I was close to Mr.Grant. He had three dogs, all different species and all so small and cute. After his…death, it's me who has been looking after them." He looked at Muriel and smiled but it was pretty evident that he missed Mr.Grant. I guess he knew it too, but did no attempt to hide it.

"How did you meet Morgan?" asked Layla. All heads turned to my side, except Muriel's. She was busy looking through the binocular at the house but I knew she was listening.

"I met her in my eighth grade. She shared biology classes with me. I was struggling to find a lab partner so she told me that she would be mine. Since then we used to hang out pretty much every day and then somewhere along the way…it happened."

"It…happened, huh?" asked Aiden, smiling.

"Shut up. I …"

Muriel cut through me, "I think something is wrong. There are a lot of people."

We all got hold of a binocular each and looked. Muriel was right, something was definitely wrong. There were a lot of people, gathered around here and there, many more coming. A lump filled my throat as I took in what I saw.

"People", my voice was just loud enough for them to hear, "We missed it. We are too late now"

*****

We walked towards the house in silence. I had mixed emotions running through my mind. We could have warned Mathew. We could have told his mother that she might be in danger. In our small moment of happiness, we had forgotten about others, their lives and their families. We, for a matter of seconds, became selfish. But we also lost a chance to understand what that bear-like thing is. We should have paid attention. We couldn't rescue the lady from her death like superheroes nor could we rescue ourselves from the mental turmoil we were all going through. None of us spoke since getting out of the abandoned building, the silence among us filled with things we couldn't speak about. The hot afternoon was turning into a mild evening, my favorite time of the day. It was the time when even the biggest star in our galaxy was taking a break, something that I terribly needed. We pushed through people, their sweat filling my nostrils and their whispers filling my ears. We decided to find Mathew, to comfort him, knowing clearly that this would do nothing to help him whatsoever. We found him after some time, sitting between some people we did not know, tears running down his face as he looked at his mother, lying there with no life in her. Deciding to not break into their privacy, we turned around and I met a pair of bright blue eyes, staring at me critically, eyes that looked exactly like mine.

"Sam…wha…what are you doing here?" asked Brianna looking at all of us. "What are you all doing here?"

I swallowed. "Brianna, come let's talk outside." I said, grabbing hold of her by her shoulder and leading her out of the house, the others following us.

*****

"Sam, I know there is no way for you to know that lady and no way at all to know her children. Then how the hell are you here?" she was standing still like a statue, her hands folded, but her eyes looked at me disapprovingly. We had taken her to the abandoned building but she did not seem to be paying attention to her surroundings. "I have been ignoring your weird behavior for a really long time now, but I can't do that anymore. What the hell is going on?"

"Listen, we would…" Evan began but Brianna cut him off, or rather shouted at him.

"Oh, shut your stupid mouth, guy, I am taking to him." She pointed at me accusingly. Evan opened his mouth to say something to score back but I shut him up.

"Evan, let it go. Brianna, listen to me. I would like to tell this to you more than to anyone but this is too complicated and I don't want to drag you into this and you might even think that I had turned crazy. Please just understand. I want to…"

"Then do it. Tell her." Muriel's voice rose.

"I am sorry, what?" I said, looking at her in disbelief.

Muriel sighed and said, "She was the one who helped us figure out things when none of us had the common sense to do it. She never bothered you by asking why you were hanging out with random people. She helped you get through a dark time after Morgan's death. She deserves to know the truth, Samuel."

I looked at Muriel and wished that she wasn't this straight forward and still be so true. And I knew she was right, Brianna deserved to know it all. But I couldn't tell her. That would involve a lot of emotions and how at different times, I had to lie to her and still not feel sorry about it, even when she was being the best sister anyone could ask for. I looked over at Muriel and she nodded her head, as if she knew what I was thinking and spoke up.

"Brianna let's go for a walk. I promise to tell you everything."

*****

Brianna was not just the stylish, famous girl I thought she was. She was not just the sweet, calm and supportive sister she had become for me. She was strong, fierce and equally brave and that was something I was not expecting. I always saw her as my little sister, who was still the small girl who clung on to me whenever we saw scary movies as kids. She had not seemed like a mature person to me and needless to say I never treated her like one. But now I see how senseless all that was. She grew up to be someone with a strong perspective and a girl whose views were not just the musings of a sixteen-year-old teenage girl. And it was only when Muriel helped me, did I notice how much she grew. Muriel and Brianna came back after what felt like a lifetime. Muriel just walked in casually, smiling and talking with Brianna. I stood there not knowing what to say or do, but no one seemed to consider that I was embarrassed for not knowing my sister well, so I just pretended like they did.

"So, what you said sounded like something you guys made up but I believe you for some weird reason" said Brianna, sitting beside Evan and trying really hard not to meet my eyes. "And I have something that might help you, but before that, I am sorry that I shouted at you, Evan. It's just... I hate when people lie to me or not include me in things because they think I am too small. Also, I can seriously lose my temper sometimes."

Evan smiled, "That's fine, I, of all people can understand temper issues." Brianna smiled.

"So, as I was saying, I have something that might help you. I don't know if this is valid but I know a lot about that lady. The boy, Mathew, is my friend and he is pretty talkative so I know a bit about his mother. She did not particularly have any friends because she was a different kind of thinker and she was not interested in the small talks most people engage in. She got divorced a year and a half before and they did not have a proper family life. She is pretty close with her neighbor, I don't know his name, but they were good friends. She was respected by many people though, including my parents, who knew her, because of some theories and articles she used to write in the newspaper. She is…was a woman with knowledge." She finished.

"Wow you have a pretty good memory skill." Aiden said, looking impressed.

"Well, if you hear this every once in a week while sitting in a boring history lecture, then it's not very easy to forget, is it?" she shrugged.

"History is something we don't discuss. It's that stupid assignment that led us here." grumbled Evan.

"I don't think so, Evan; even if we did not have the assignment, there would have been some way or the other that we would have ended up here. Seems like this whole bizarre thing was made for us." said Layla.

"So, what now?" I spoke up, knowing that I couldn't keep silent for long.

"The only thing I know is that I am too tired to bother about anything now" said Evan and as he said it, I realized how tired each one of us looked and I felt the fatigue in me pulling me down too.

Brianna got up saying that she needed to go see Mathew and we all decided to wait for her. After she went, I sat at the far corner of the floor, my mind mushed up with thoughts that made me want to cry and kill myself at the same time. I was staring at the small dots of people at Mathew's house when Muriel came and sat beside me.

"Do you think I did the right thing?" I asked as soon as she sat down. "Do you think letting her into this was right? Or am I just being an over protective brother?"

"You are being an over protective brother, but yes, I think you did the right thing. You don't understand how bad it is to not have someone in your family that you can't openly talk to" she said it and I believed her, because I knew that she was not the kind of person who would lie to make me feel better. "I live in a house with my father and sister but I bet they don't even know what my favorite food is." she shrugged.

"Ok, two things. One…you have a sister? And how come I don't know?" I asked, turning around to face her. She wore the scarf around her neck, the horses in it bright from the city lights. She laughed and said "Yes, I have a sister. Her name is Clint, she is eighteen years old and is in college now. And you don't know because I didn't tell you. Well, apparently, we have a long shot at being best friends. So, what's the second thing?"

I felt a warmth rise in me as I heard her call me her best friend. I liked them all but I knew that I had something with Muriel that I did not have with the others.

"Well, the second thing is…what *is* your favorite food?" I asked, grinning. She smiled her beautiful smile "It's pizza. What is yours?"

"Hmm let me think. Ice cream probably…it helps me "cool down"" I said. She looked at me and raised her eyebrows. "You didn't get the irony, did you?"

"Sam, I don't think that's how the concept of irony works." She said, clearly trying to hide her grin. I shook my head and then slowly the others joined us and we just sat there, enjoying what we had right now, beneath all those layers of guilt and disbelief and tiredness, something which we all knew would be hard to find in the future; peace.

CHAPTER NINE

"Brianna…"

"I don't want to talk to you." she said, rushing up the stairs.

"Please, Brianna…" I ran after her into her room and stopped on my tracks. The room did not look at all like it was before. All sides of the walls were plain and simple except the one that faced the bed; it was filled with caricatures, paintings, and random pencil drawings.

"You…you can draw." Which seemed like a ridiculous thing to say since I was standing there and looking at her work.

"Guess you don't know your sister well huh?"

"Ok listen to me. I know it was wrong for me to shut you out after everything you did for me…"

"And the realization hits now?!" she started pacing the room back and forth, her eyes trained on me. "Sam, I might have a lot of friends but that does not mean that I have people I can confide in. For a long time, I had no one I could openly talk to and I thought that maybe you could help me. But then you became this weird person altogether and you acted like I didn't even exist."

"That's not true." I said, feeling the anger boil in me.

"Oh, really? Then tell me one time were we actually spent time together before all of this happened. Don't have to rack your brains for it Sam; you won't be able to give one because there isn't any. Unlike others, I just thought you would be different, that you would actually understand me and here you are repeating the ordinary."

I wanted to yell at her for blaming me for the things I didn't even know. But somewhere, deep down, I could feel the hurt as I realized I had let down someone I loved, yet again. "I…" my voice barely came out. "Being me was not my choice. I know you are sad because I did not realize the real person you are. But have you realized who I really am?"

"Sam, listen to me…" she began.

"NO, you listen to me this time." I shouted "I am not justifying how I treated you, but do you think that I would have ignored you if we had a real conversation?"

"So you are saying it's all my fault now?" She asked, tears gushing down her eyes.

"That is not what I meant. Don't read between the lines."

"That's exactly what you are saying, Sam."

"Then you don't know me at all. Nice work, Brianna." I said and walked out of her room, slamming the door behind me.

*****

It was Monday morning and we had gathered around to have breakfast.

"What happened to you two?" mom eyed us suspiciously.

"Yeah you both look like wet dogs." Dad said, sipping the juice.

Brianna made no attempt to talk to me so neither did I. The cold anger from our argument had faded away to be replaced by a strong feeling of hurt.

"Well, anyway…" my dad spoke up, clearly to start a conversation. "I couldn't sleep well last night."

"Why? What happened? I asked, fear rising in me. 'Couldn't sleep last night' was not something that I wanted to hear anymore.

"Umm...because I wasn't sleepy. Why do you both seem so tensed about it?" he asked, his bright blue eyes swinging from me to Brianna.

"Nothing." We both said together.

"Why are you both behaving so weirdly?" asked my mom, adjusting her hands on her hip, looking like a forty two-year old version of Brianna.

"I want to get to school. I have an assignment to submit. Bye." I ran out of the house and I could hear Brianna shouting excuses to run away too. Today was the day Mr.Beckham was supposed to return and we had to submit the assignment. As soon as I reached school, I scanned the crowd for my friends. They were standing near the history classroom, not bothering to enter.

"Mr.Beckham is not returning until next month." Aiden said, as I approached them.

"Where is Brianna?" asked Evan.

"How would I know?" I snapped. I saw Muriel looked at me vaguely and averted my gaze. "So we have a free hour, what do we do?"

"I have a free hour too. Do you guys mind me joining you?" Brianna spoke from behind me.

"Not at all, you are one of us now." Layla said.

Brianna smiled. "Then I need to tell you people something. Come on."

*****

"This is our old school bathroom." Brianna sat down on one of the window ledges, brushing away the dust and I didn't even bother asking how she knew this place. The place was covered with cobwebs, discarded bottles, and toiletries. I turned a broken bathtub upside down and Muriel, me, and Aiden sat down on it while Evan and Layla sat on both sides of Brianna. Why we had a bathtub in school will be one of the biggest mysteries of all time.

"Ok here's the thing. This is just a theory and I don't know if it makes sense but anyway…according to what you guys said, all of them, at least the ones we know, have seen this bear like thing and experienced sleep paralysis and next day or sometime soon they die, right?" asked Brianna. We all shook our heads in agreement, she stared into the distance for some time, "Then, you have been looking at the wrong place."

The hurt in me took advantage. "So, you are saying that we practically spent all of this time doing something that was not right? Well, that's encouraging." Brianna glared at me, her bright blue eyes staring accusingly at mine.

"Hey, from what we have seen, things didn't go well between you both" said Evan, showing a time out sign "So both of you cut each other some slack and Brianna, please continue." I looked at Evan and raised an eyebrow and he looked away, flustered.

"Thank you Evan." Brianna continued. "Ok see, that day you were at Mathew's house after his mom suffered from this sleep thing because if not he wouldn't have seen the…what's it?"

"Bean nighe." Layla said.

"Yeah, bean nighe. Which means that seeing the bean nighe happens either before or after the sleep paralysis but the creature that they all saw was when they were experiencing sleep paralysis, not when they died. So if you have to see the creature…"

"We have to find the people who are going to suffer sleep paralysis" finished Aiden.

"Find its next victim" said Muriel "That makes sense." Brianna looked happy that she could help and everyone smiled and nodded their heads appreciatively. It indeed was a good observation but I was so angry at her that I couldn't bring myself to appreciate her, although I had a lot of back-stabbing remarks. I bit back a retort and spoke up, "OK, but how exactly do we find these so called next victims?"

"Is there some pattern of how the deaths are happening? thing similar in their locality or something?" asked Brianna.

"No, I looked it up a few days ago." Aiden said, shaking his head. "It all happened in random places at random times. Nothing is similar, as far as I know." We all sat in silence for a while, thinking and racking our brains for something that might help. The bell rang, muffled by all the trees around us. We gathered our bags and walked back to our classes.

"Sam, what are you doing? Brianna is helping us." Muriel said, taking hold of my hand in the hallway crowd.

"I am not doing anything."

"Sam."

"Muriel."

"Oh, no." Layla said, her face spotting something in the crowd of students, "Let's go the other way around." She started pushing us in the opposite direction when a harsh voice cut through the corridor.

"Layla, running away?" we all turned around to face a muscular guy, with close cropped hair and pale complexion. I recognized him immediately because it was pretty hard to forget the face of someone who made your middle school terrible.

"Florence Patt."

"Ahhh…such a long time it has been, Samuel. How pleasant to see all my old friends in one place. But excuse me, I just wanted to talk to my girl." He said, looking at Layla.

"*My* girl?" asked Evan, looking from Layla to Florence. "I am not his girl", she said, the color rushing into her face.

"Oh but you are now, since your freak pink-haired friend is no longer there". He said, as his friends scooted and howled behind him.

"Leave her alone Patt, go look for someone else who is ready to lick your feet." Muriel said, standing in between Layla and Florence.

"Oh, Oh, look at you, all big and funny. If she doesn't want to be, then why don't you give it a try?" he said, looking at her and smiling.

"Leave her out of this, Florence." Layla said, pushing Muriel out of the path, "Like I said a million times already, you are wasting your time. I am not interested in you. So take a hint and leave!"

"Oh, how brave. But what do I do…you are not getting rid of me anytime soon." He moved closer to her. Before I could think about the consequences, I punched his face, the anger of all he did to me when I was small and his ruthless behavior to Layla, dictating my action. Blood gushed down his nose and he bent down, his hands cupped around it. His friends ran to his aid, some came over to us, with a clear you-want-to-fight-come-let's-fight look.

"Ok guys, you want to fight someone, how about me?" Evan inched forward with a threatening glare in his eye. Students gathered around us, looking curiously. "I am not that bad, you might remember, don't you?" he asked, pointing to the one in the middle.

"Well, I can help you with it Evan, Sam you in?" asked Aiden coming forward. His hands were shivering beside him, but I appreciated the effort.

"Totally." I replied.

"I am not bad either, want to try?" asked Muriel, tying her loose hair back up.

"I am totally in." said Brianna, her eyes challenging anyone to come forward. To be truthful, Evan and Brianna looked like they might kill you if you even leave a breath out. Signs of 'can be a great couple', I suppose.

"No one is fighting anyone" said Mr.Andrew, pushing kids out of his way and standing between us. "All of you, detention after school. Now back to class, kids."

The crowd started thinning and Florence's friends led him away. Finally, we were the only ones left. "That guy has been bothering me for a while." Layla murmured.

"Seems like he won't be doing it again anytime soon." I said, taking my bag from the floor.

"You, my friend, have got style." Aiden said, winking at me.

"And if you are not planning to keep his blood as a memorial or something, then please wash your hands." said Muriel, crinkling. We all walked to class and I felt it again, the bond that binds us together, the friendship we shared and I knew that some things were worth an apology and a second chance. I put my hands around Brianna's shoulder and smiled at her, she looked back and both of our eyes spoke a million apologizes that words would never have been able to express.

CHAPTER TEN

"If you have finished, you may go." Mr.Andrew's voice rang through the silent classroom. The six of us had spent the last half an hour writing 'fighting people is bad' one hundred times, even though it should have been 'fighting bad people is good'. We all gave the papers to Mr.Andrew and shuffled out of class. "So where are we headed?" asked Muriel.

"I am hungry" said Evan, rubbing his stomach, "Brim's?" we all shook our heads in agreement and walked over to the parking lot. As we were walking, Evan's stomach let out a grumbling noise as if to prove that he really was hungry and we all started teasing him when we heard a voice behind us. "Muriel" I turned around to find a handsome guy, maybe twenty, running towards us, his messy black hair jumping up and down.

"Hey." Muriel greeted him, "What are you doing here?"

"I came to see some of his teachers to invite them for the prayer. You still not coming?"

"I…I'll think about it. Oh, these are my friends." She said, eager to change the topic, whatever it was. "This is Rease's brother, Ryan and Ryan, these are my friends." He nodded and smiled at us. "Actually" he said, pulling out a card from his bag. "We are having a prayer service for Rease, it's been almost a month. It's on next Sunday, at the church. If you guys can make it, it'll mean a lot." A month.

"Yeah sure, we will be there." Layla said. And we all agreed.

*****

The chocolate shake was amazing, so was the pizza, mood…not so much. "So, tell me again, why exactly are you not going for this prayer service?" asked Aiden.

"Like I already said, I am not going because I don't want to. I don't believe in this kind of stuff. Is it that hard to follow, big brained guy?" Muriel looked like she might kill the next person who asked this question again.

"Muriel, we know you don't believe in this kind of stuff, but wouldn't it mean something to Rease and his family if you went?" asked Layla.

"Muriel, I don't know if this is any of my business but…" said Brianna, her hands absently rotating her straw in the shake, "…Is there some other reason that is holding you back?" Muriel looked at me and we both exchanged a glance and I nodded; it was about time for them to know.

"OK, here's the thing. Rease and his family… we were close and they were pretty kind and helpful to us after my mom passed away. Me and him…we pretty much grew up together. Well, one day, he said that he liked me which made things a bit complicated and awkward between us, but then we never talked about it. Not until a week before his death." She said, her stare fixed on the table.

"Let me guess, you liked him." Evan asked, a small smile tugging at the corner of his lips.

"Well, I don't know…maybe. He knew almost everything about me, how could I not?" she shrugged. "But the conversation we had, didn't go too well. We had not been in good terms for a while and then all of this happened." "I didn't get to say anything to him" she added a second later. There was silence all around the table and no one seemed to know what to say.

"Muriel, you might not believe in all this stuff. I mean, I get how you are feeling." I said. "But this has nothing to do with what you believe in, it's about Rease because I know that if I got a chance like this, I would use it to show how sorry I am. Not that it would change anything." Muriel stirred her shake casually but from the way her eyes looked, it was evident that she was deep in thought. For a while, no one spoke and a wave of cool air flowed into the café as someone came inside. Instinctively, all the heads turned towards the door but it was just another high schooler, enjoying a normal evening. I didn't even know what normal meant anymore.

"Fine, I'll go." Said Muriel, slumping back in her chair, "But only if you people join me."

"Great, we'll be there", said Layla, looking happy about it.

*****

"Black or white?" Brianna stood in front of her wardrobe, different kinds of clothes strewn all over the floor while I lay sprawled on the bed, staring blankly at the ceiling. My eyes travelled from the ceiling to the paintings that adorned the wall. Suddenly, a black cloth fell on my face and I sat up, pulling it away, "What?"

"Ok, daydreamer, black or white?" she held up two dresses close to her shoulders and looked at me expectantly.

"Uhhh…white, I guess. Cause it's not a funeral, so black might seem a bit odd."

"OK then white it is." she said grandly, hurriedly throwing the rest of the dresses into the wardrobe. "What about you? What are you wearing?"

"Is that Morgan?"

"What?"

"That picture", I said, pointing at the one in the middle, "Is that Morgan?" Brianna slid into the bed beside me and looked at the picture with her wide, blue eyes. "Yes" her voice was nearly a whisper. I looked at the painting, the lines that made her flowing hair and eyes that looked like it had never seen a dull moment.

I realized with a start, from the way the color looked among the other drawings, that it was new.

"You miss her." I meant it as a question but it came out more like a statement. She nodded her head slightly and let out a sigh. "She…we were…you know…pretty close." I looked over at Brianna and saw that her eyes glazed from the tears she held back. She was strong, stronger than I imagined but she was broken too, just like we all were and suddenly, I feared if all of this was too much for her. I took her hand in mine. "The drawing… it looks beautiful." She smiled at me and then fixed her gaze on the picture.

"Brianna?"

"Yeah?"

"If there is anything you feel like talking about, you can always come to me, you know that right?" she tore her gaze from the wall and looked at me. "Yeah, I know" she whispered.

"So," she said, standing up, "What are you wearing?"

"I have no idea"

She smiled. "You might not know, Samuel Colton, but I definitely do."

Half an hour later, Brianna came out of her room and stared at me like an artist appreciating her own work. "See, I told you grey was your color. It makes your eyes stand out." I was wearing a black corduroy jacket over a grey shirt, tucked into a pair of black pants. I knew that I looked different, maybe even good and that Brianna was right about her choice. But if I had any chance of getting any attention, Brianna took that all away. She looked incredible in her plain white dress that hung down till her knees. Her hair was left open and her feet were covered in grey strapped high heeled shoes. "Why are you looking at me like that?" she asked.

"You look good. Evan might explode today." I said, trying hard to cover the grin. She laughed sarcastically. "He is a nice guy, maybe I might give it a go." She stuck her tongue out and this time it was my chance to laugh out. "Isn't he a bit old for you?"

"He is *your* age, Sam." She said walking down the stairs. "And actually, we must stop by his house. That's where we all agreed to meet."

"You both look amazing." Mom sat in the armchair, sipping coffee as we reached the bottom. "What's the occasion?"

"We are going to prayer service for one of my…"I hesitated, trying to find the right word. "School-mates."

"Be careful and come on time." She yelled from behind us as we walked towards the bike. "Sam, on second thoughts, why don't we walk?" said Brianna, eyeing the bicycles. "It might be more comfortable."

"For you." I said but put the keys back into my pocket as we started walking towards the Miles' Manor.

It just took us ten minutes to reach Evan's place. The house was decorated in an ancient style, with dark colors and intricate patterns. It spread across a whole lot of land, with gardens and a long backyard. Ms.Miles invited us into an aesthetic and royal looking dining hall, a long wooden table in the middle of the room. The surface of the table had carvings of flowers and patterns at the edges and the seats of the chairs were made of red velvet plush cloth. One look around and I knew that Layla would love this place. "So, what do you think, Brianna?"

She snickered and said, "It's a bit too much for my taste."

"What's a bit too much for your taste?"

Evan stepped down the winding staircase like a prince descending down for a royal ceremony. Brianna smiled awkwardly, "Uh…I meant…Sam's dressing today." She said pointing at me. "Your house looks nice." She added which seemed completely out of place.

"Thanks and I think you look dope man." He said, smiling. "You, as usual, look good." he said, looking over at Brianna, clearly not hiding his interest he had in her.

"Thanks." I said quickly, just to remind them that I was still here. "You look good too." And he did. He wore a light pink tuxedo with a white shirt, which made his pale complexion even more pale and he looked stripped out of color except for his flaming red hair and his deep black eyes. We sat around the table, the cushions surprisingly comfortable, and talked for a while, when the bell rang and Layla and Aiden came in. Both of them looked good, Aiden in his black shirt and grey pants and Layla in her buttery-yellow frock.

"Where's Muriel?" Aiden asked, as he sat beside me. "She'll come, won't she?"

And as if to answer it, the doorbell rang the second time and we all turned around to find Muriel walking in looking…normal. She wore a blue ankle length jeans and sneakers and a t-shirt that read "American Scotts".

"American Scotts? Really?" asked Brianna, rolling her eyes.

"What?" asked Muriel, looking down at the t-shirt. Slowly her eyes travelled across us and she raised an eyebrow, "Am I missing something?"

"Muriel, aren't you a bit casual for the occasion?" asked Aiden.

"Casual and kind of inappropriate." added Evan.

"See, my dear fellow companions, I wore this because, (a)I have no idea what to wear, (b) I own a really low amount of dresses, because I use it rarely and (c) my parents ARE American-Scottish." She fixed her hands on her hips, as if that explained everything.

"My parents are half-Americans too, but we don't wear t-shirts that say so to the prayer service of a friend." Brianna said, shaking her head slightly.

"Yeah, my parents too." I added.

"Uhh…that was quite evident, since you know… she's your sister." Evan shrugged. "Right" I murmured.

"Ok, but we are running late, so why don't we just go and end this thing. I am even supposed to say something and I am pretty sure that it sucks to the core." Muriel sighed heavily.

"I have a plan" said Brianna. "You always do" I said.

"Yeah, well…" she rose from her seat and went over to Muriel. "…my house is just a few minutes away and I am fairly your size, so…you know what I mean."

"Don't even think about it" whispered Muriel, while the rest of us shouted, "Cool."

"I can come with you guys" said Layla. They pushed a not-so-happy-looking Muriel out of the house and left the three of us behind.

"Hey, I have to feed the dogs, you want to come?" asked Evan. The three of us walked the length of the lawn and reached a fence that separated his house from Mr.Grant's. He reached over the fence and unlocked a small door on the right end and stepped into the lawn of the other house. He took a turn to the left, towards the rear of the house and grabbed a bag of food that sat at the corner of a wall.

"So, how many are there?" asked Aiden.

"Three. Two Labrador and a Golden Retriever" Evan said, absently. He leaned down on the cages and whistled slightly as he opened them and let the dogs free. The dogs looked healthy and well fed and the golden retriever's skin shined bright in the morning sunlight.

"Here, have these" murmured Evan, so smoothly and with so much care that it was hard to believe that he had said it. Suddenly and without much thinking, the words flew out of my mouth. "So, what's up with you and Brianna?"

Evan stood up straight as if someone pulled him right out of the ground. "What?"

"Don't pretend like you don't know what he is talking about" said Aiden, a smile tugging at the end of his lips. "We all have eyes and ears, you know."

"Uhh…I…It's…" Evan looked like the most uncomfortable guy in the world. I couldn't hold my laugh in any longer, so I laughed out loud, startling Evan. "Man, she is my sister and I know that she has quite an effect on guys. It's fine."

"I really like Brianna. I was afraid to ask her since my experience in this field is pretty bad." He said, his face the same color as his tux.

"You? Afraid?" asked Aiden, smirking. "Wow, today is the best day of my life."

I laughed, then steadied my voice and said, "Evan, I am fine with it if she's ok about it too." Evan nodded his head so fast that I thought it might come apart.

"And she happens to like paintings very much, ones that hide deep meanings in it" I added. Evan blushed, maybe for the first and the last time, and then hurriedly bent down to look at the dogs. Aiden winked at me and I smiled back.

"So…" Aiden asked, "Does Mr.Grant have any kids?"

"No" said Evan, looking relieved by the change of topic, "He never got married. He was a non-believer and at his time it was not such an acceptable thing. And he was not ready to give up in his ideals for just marrying someone."

"Sounds like Allen and Mr.Grant might have got well together", murmured Aiden. After some time, Evan's mom called out to us saying that the girls were back. We hurriedly filled the cages with enough food and water, locked the dogs up and headed back home.

"So…"Evan said. "…don't say anything to Brianna. Not now, ok?"

"OK" we both said together. We were climbing up the stairs when Muriel came through the doorway. She looked…beautiful. She always was, but this time she looked elegantly beautiful, completely unlike her. She wore a baby blue sleeveless dress that ran till her toes; her bushy black hair lay down her shoulders. Her eyes were lined under her spectacles and she resembled a blue sky on a bright day.

"Jesus" sighed Evan. "What did they do to you?"

"Ok I know I look ridiculous." She puffed her cheeks and rolled her eyes.

"Ridiculous?" said Evan, as if he couldn't believe his ears, "Did you look at yourself in a mirror or something?"

"You look pretty." I said, my voice low. Layla and Brianna came out of the house and sniggered at the looks on our faces.

"Day just keeps getting better and better." Aiden smiled.

"Shall we go? We are already late." Layla said, glancing down at her watch. We hurried down the stairs and started walking towards the church. The road was bright but not hot, a pleasant climate.

"Wait." Muriel said from behind. "You have something in your hair." She pulled out a twig and threw it down the path. Layla was speaking to someone on the phone and Aiden was trying really hard to take a good picture of the trees above but he seemed to have no luck. Evan and Brianna walked side by side, both of them laughing and talking.

"They look good together." Muriel said, following my gaze.

"Yeah."

"You ok with it?" she asked.

"Hmmm…I guess, I mean it's really not my right to say who she should date or not."

"You're her brother."

I grinned, "Exactly why." She let out an annoyed groan. "This is the most uncomfortable thing I have ever worn."

"Hey, you look good." I said.

"Yeah well, you want to see something?" I nodded my head and she slightly lifted her dress to reveal her feet and saw that she was still wearing the sneakers she wore earlier. I burst out laughing and she looked annoyed but she was trying hard not to laugh too. "Come on, it's not that bad, is it?"

"Not at all. If someone asks you about it, say you tried a fusion…combo…something trend." I said, smiling widely.

"Sure. I will tell them I tried a fusion…combo… something trend." she said, mimicking my voice. "But actually the sneakers are least of my worries." She said after a pause.

"What's the first?"

"The eulogy." She pulled out a piece of folded paper from her dress pocket- wow they had pockets- and slowly turned it in her hands. "I am really bad at this. When I asked my dad what to write, he said that for my mom's funeral he had spoken what she would have wanted to hear, which was a completely vague and cryptic answer."

"I am sure he'll love it." I said.

"Well, I am not sure about that" her eyes slowly filled with tears and one ran down her freckled cheek and I realized that more than anything else, she did not want to come because she dreaded having to relive the pain she tried so hard to forget, just like me. I put my arm around her shoulder and squeezed her. "Muriel, I am so sorry. It was stupid of me not to realize why you didn't want to come."

"It's ok." She said, wiping her eyes. "Did I ruin my eyeliner?"

"A bit." I said.

"Ok Brianna will kill me so we are going to say that you smudged it."

"What?" I said, "How would I do that, by rubbing you in the eye for fun?!"

"Hmm", she whispered with a small smile, "Interesting theory." I smiled and she smiled her beautiful smile back at me. "Ok so I might probably cry and I am one hundred percent sure I messed up the eulogy, so not such a good day."

"But…" I said, pointing at her dress, "On the bright side, you have pockets in your dress."

*****

The church backyard was filled with chairs covered in white cloth. Small white flowers lined the sides of the yard, giving it a heavenly and pleasing look. We met Ryan and his parents, Muriel's sister and father, and settled beside them almost near the front. The Priest prayed for a while and Rease's parents and brother presented their eulogy. After them another guy from our school spoke for a while. I looked around and found out that many of the kids I knew were here. Rease seemed like a fun and outgoing guy, seeing that so many people had arrived here for him. I was so immersed in thinking about how he would have been if I had known him alive that it startled me when I heard Muriel's name being called out.

"…his closest friend…Muriel Payton."

Muriel looked paler than usual, making her freckles look more pronounced. She stumbled her way up to the podium, spread the sheet of paper on the platform and looked around at the crowd for a minute, taking it all in. Then she tucked a stray strand of hair behind her ear, took a deep breath and began, "Rease was my best friend. Thinking back, I don't remember a time where I did not know him. I don't remember a time where I went to school without him. He was a great guy, even though he liked blueberry yoghurt that make most people turn away because of its smell. He was an amazing friend, even though he rarely took showers saying that water was depleting on earth and it was essential to preserve it."

A small laugh spread through the crowd and I found myself smiling, noticing that she spoke with so much warmth.

"And I know for a fact that if he was here, he would run around and shout in people's ear that all of this made no sense. Rease was that one person everyone in this world needs, that one person who would always be by your side. And yet, here I am, not being able to be with that one person the world gave me." Her voice broke.

"I have read somewhere that the day you love someone most is the day you lose them. I have also read somewhere that you should never hold back whatever you have to say to someone because it might be too late when you want to. I never understood what they meant, but now I do. There are a million things I want to tell him but I can't and I never will. I never had much faith in anything but I know one thing for sure. I had faith in him and will always have faith in him and there will be a place in my life that can never be filled, a hollow space that the person I loved the most left behind." After a long silence, she whispered a small thank you, not raising her eyes up to meet the crowd. Tears ran down her cheeks as she gathered the paper and slowly walked towards the church and away from the backyard. I got up to follow her, but Layla pulled me down shaking her head slightly, "Give her some time, we will find her after this."

As the service continued, something in Muriel's speech stayed behind in my mind and I racked my brains hard to find what it was without much success. I thought about Morgan and how my life had turned upside down since she left. The pain I felt every time I thought about her squeezed my insides. I thought about how Muriel said that she would never be the same anymore, how she felt that hollow void in her. Every single one of us felt it and more people would, if this continued and I was overcome with a wave of longing for no one to go through what me and my friends had experienced. And for that, we needed to do something. We, a bunch of seventeen-year-olds, had to do something.

*****

We found Muriel at the back end, surrounded by a pile of the construction material for a new section of the church. She sat on the stairs, with her legs propped on top of a pile of iron rods, her hair flying in the light breeze.

"Not a word." She whispered as we came close. "I swear if you say something I'll throw those rod things straight into your skull. So, if you don't want to look like a cheap unicorn, don't say anything."

"Well, we haven't said a word since we came here, *you* have been doing all the talking" said Evan as he sat beside her. Muriel shrugged and we all sat around her on the stairs.

"Your father has been looking for you." Brianna said, her eyes full of concern.

"Well, I am going back home so he can see me then. And it's not me who ruined the eyeliner, it was your brother. He rubbed on my eyes." she said, smiling crookedly.

"Hey" I protested, "She didn't even ask about that." Muriel looked at me, grinning, then her eyes travelled around the church, "Wow, this place is so quiet."

"You don't come here often, do you?" asked Layla. Muriel looked at Layla and raised an eyebrow and muttered something like "stupid question to ask me."

"I am just curious, ok?" said Aiden, as he turned around to face Muriel. "What made you not believe in any of this?"

"Well..." She said, "...speaking matter-of-factly, we all know that the biggest bloodsheds in history is due to this. And besides, there is no scientific proof. Speaking personally, I do believe in God, but the God I worship is in the goodness in humans, the kindness they show, the humanitarian concepts they own. When Layla said that story of believers killing people because they didn't believe in God, I just can't understand how God would approve to that. Now we see people killing each other, hurting and murdering without a second thought. So, I just don't think that God dwells where good doesn't exist. As Dan Brown said, 'religion is flawed because mankind is flawed.'"

I had read it before; 'religion is flawed because mankind is flawed'. At that instant, the idea popped into my head so quickly that I thought I heard a faint click. Morgan would have said what Muriel just told now. I thought about what I heard Evan say about Mr.Grant, "He was a non-believer and at his time it was not such an acceptable thing." And Aiden had said… "Sounds like Allen and Mr.Grant might have got well together". My mind raced back to what Brianna had said about Mathew's mom, "She did not particularly have any friends because she was a different kind of thinker". And what Muriel said about Rease, "And I know for a fact that if he was here, he would run around and shout in people's ear that all of this made no sense." It fit in, all of it.

"Hey", I said and saw all the heads turn towards me, "I think I just found a pattern."

PART THREE

"I need a father,

I need a mother,

I need some older, wiser being to cry to.

I talk to God,

But the sky is empty."

– Sylvia Plath

CHAPTER ELEVEN

"Oh Gods!"

"This…why…how?! I don't understand." Brianna looked like someone had slapped her on the face, but she looked better than the rest of them. "Answer me."

"I am not really sure what your question is." I said, my voice sounding far away.

"How did you figure this out?"

"Well…"I began, "…think about it. Morgan did not believe in any of this. Nor did Mr.Grant. What about Allen?" Aiden slowly nodded his head to confirm. "See… Muriel, Rease was a non-believer too, right? And what about Jocelyn, Layla?"

"You are right" murmured Layla.

"Yeah, Rease too. But how is this possible? Why is this happening?" asked Muriel, her hands clenching together.

"I don't know how, but look at it. No common location, no particular connection among any of them, nothing. This is the only thing that ties them together. And it creepily matches what Layla said about La Iglesia de Muerta por Dentro."

"God, we need a smaller name" muttered Evan. I dismissed what he said and continued, "The only difference is, here they ceased to believe, there they believed, but were against it."

"Hold on a second" said Aiden, his eyes filled with doubt and confusion. "This might be a possible pattern, maybe the only connection we can find. Let's think about what we need to do next. We can't let anyone else lose their life."

"Find the prey." Layla whispered. Then she cleared her voice and said louder, "We need to find the prey. Brianna said the other day that in order to find out and stop this we need to find its next target and if it is following this pattern, it is not going to be an easy job. There are almost hundreds of people around us that don't believe in this stuff. It can be anyone, not to mention, it can easily be one of us."

"You are right, but there must be something we can do. We can't just sit here and wait for something to happen" said Evan, rising to his feet. "The story about the church matches the situation, so maybe, there might be something in it that we missed the first time." He started pacing around as the silence settled in. Think, I whispered to myself, there has to be something.

"The bear" whispered Aiden.

"What about it?" asked Brianna.

"They all saw a bear, right? No one knows what killed the people in that old church. What if it was that bear?"

"But they saw the bear." said Muriel.

"YEAH, WE HEARD THAT" said Evan, a little impatiently. "Sorry, nerves", he quickly added.

"Listen, if it's the bear that caused the deaths then we wouldn't know about it. They all saw the bear and died the next day, which means whatever caused the death was something we still have no idea about" explained Muriel.

"Thanks, you just made things far more complicated" murmured Aiden.

"And clear" said Brianna. "Think about it, they saw the bear and they died the next day."

"Why do you guys keep repeating that like brand new information?" said Evan, making no effort to hide his impatience. The dread and fear that was slowly creeping in made it hard for all of us to concentrate. Brianna let out an impatient noise and continued, "Think about it. What if the bear is the reason after all? What if it did something that affected them that led to their deaths?"

"We need to find the bear." I said with finality. I knew that one way or another, the answers to all our questions lay with this so called 'bear'.

*****

Two hours. That's how long we spent going through every single article the internet could give us about sleep paralysis and myths that surrounded it but, without even a slight ray of hope. Exhausted sighs and frustrated groans filled the room. We all looked at each other, the despair, fear, and hopelessness filling the five pairs of eyes that I stared into. A light knock woke all of us up and we turned to see my mother walk into the room with some rolls and juices.

"Eat something kids. You all look hungry." She smiled as she set the tray down. "So, what is this assignment about?"

"It's about…" I began, but Layla spoke up.

"It's about the culture and myths of our place, Ms.Colton. We are researching on this church, La Iglesia de Muerta por Dentro. It's a bit far away from here, but it's a good place to do an assignment about."

I was going to say that it was a math assignment but whatever. My mother nodded and asked a few things about them and how they knew me. I sat awkwardly on the bed; I was not used to people talking about me to my mom. After some time my mom turned to leave but then came back, pushing the door slightly so that all we could see was her small face.

"How important is this assignment?"

"It is life and death, Ms.Colton." whispered Evan. My mom smiled like it was a joke and said, "I think you should consult one of my friends. If this assignment is really that important, then he might be able to help you people. I can see from your looks that you lot are not getting anywhere. I will send the address to Sam."

"What friend?" I asked Brianna as soon as our mom's face disappeared behind the door.

"Don't know. She has a lot" she shrugged. She was still wearing the white dress but she looked tired and pale.

"Let's eat something." I said and passed the food around.

"Maybe we could ask this friend about it" said Aiden. Arguments broke out but he waved them away and continued, "I don't mean that we have to tell him what happened but we could casually talk to him. It's not like we are getting anywhere."

"We could use some help" murmured Muriel. She had been down since the service and she tried hard to cover it. But it wasn't working, I could see it clearly and I knew the others could too.

"Yeah, I guess. We have nothing else to do." I said.

"So, we will go but before that can we sit here for a while, just take a break?" asked Layla, rubbing the back of her hands on her eyes.

"Hell, yeah" grinned Evan. "Muriel?"

"Yeah?" she looked up at him.

"Are you…hmm…are you ok?" she looked taken aback for a second but then she lowered her eyes and shook her head slowly. I slid down from the bed and went near her and the others did the same too. We gathered around Muriel as tears filled her eyes, "I am tired of being strong" she whispered. Evan moved forward and pulled her into a hug. "Yeah, we all are" he said. Layla joined the two of them, spreading her hands out to each one of us. We snuggled into each other, exhausted, scared and above all tired, tired of being responsible, tired of being fearless, tired of being strong. As the quite sobs filled the air and the afternoon light seeped in through the windows, I thought, what could be more beautiful and true than friendship?

*****

"Crap, where does this guy live?" shouted Evan, the wind making it hard to comprehend whatever he said.

"It's close" I yelled back. We were all riding along street thirty-one, the wind beating in our faces. Things turned pretty awkward as soon as we let go of each other. We fidgeted around for a while then Layla said that she wanted to change before we went, so the others went back home to change into comfortable clothes as well. Muriel stayed behind since she had left her clothes here when she changed into Brianna's dress. Once we gathered back, the awkwardness seemed to have lessened a bit. The weather had changed suddenly, the winds becoming stronger and colder and the sky turned a dark grey. It looked like it was about to rain and I was thankful for the jacket I wore. The sudden screech of tires filled the street as Layla came to a halt in front of us. If I hadn't heard the sound, I would have rode straight into her bike and things might not have ended well.

"Did we reach?" asked Muriel.

"No we are still blocks away." I replied as the six of us huddled together. "Layla, what is it?" she looked as if she saw the devil himself, the color drained from her face and I noticed that her hands were shaking on the handle of her bike.

"Layla…"

A finger rose to her lips, silencing all of us. And then she raised a shaking finger to the roof of a house. At first, I saw nothing but then something moved, something big and hairy. I let out a gasp as my brain processed what my eyes saw. It was a bear.

*****

For what felt like forever, the six of us stared at the thing, not one of us moving a finger. Then Evan spoke up, "Is it…is that…is…?"

"Yeah, maybe, I don't know." I said, my voice sounding hollow.

"What else could it be? It's not like we are living in a freaking forest." Evan said, sounding ridiculous and afraid.

"We should follow it, this is our only chance." Muriel said. She was right, this was our only chance and we couldn't lose it. Slowly, we started walking towards the thing, not bothering to take our bikes. It was sitting on top of a red bricked roof, its head turned away from us. Its whole body was covered in brown hair, except a small portion on the top of its head. It looked like an extremely hairy man with very poor hygiene.

"Stay quiet." Brianna whispered. "The last thing we want is to let it know that we are coming." The air grew colder and colder every second, the rain threatening to fall any minute. I could feel my palms sweating, the fear rising in every cell of my body and could practically hear my rapid heartbeat. Then, drop by drop, the rain started pouring down on us, making us cold to our bones. The thing sat, motionless on the roof, its hairy body becoming wetter with every passing second. Suddenly, Aiden tripped over something, falling down into a pool of water. So much for being quiet. We stopped as Aiden got up, cursing under his breath. Muriel exchanged a silent look with me, the fear clear in her eyes. I didn't want to break the gaze, every nerve in my body shouted out how wrong and dangerous this idea was, but I had no choice. I turned my head slowly and my eyes met another pair of dark, hollow ones. The thing turned its head towards where we stood, a few feet away from the house, its eyes boring into the six of us. They looked like round black balls, with no pupils and no white. The end of its puffed lips rose to the sides, the hair on its cheek rising and it took me a second to understand that it was smiling. I heard a gasp escape from one of us and I knew that nothing could be more grotesque than this sight. Then the thing got up on its legs, standing up to its full length. It was fully naked and looked like a mixture of a human and bear. It was barely 3 feet in height, its body disproportionate, its hands smaller than normal. But then it jumped to another roof, so fast that none of us realized what had happened. Without even thinking, I ran after it, my feet splashing on the wet puddles, making no attempt to be quiet. I heard someone call my name from behind and after sometime, heard footsteps following me but I did not dare look anywhere else but at that thing. It jumped from one roof to another with ease, taking its time to turn back and look at us. I ran behind it, as fast as my legs could carry me, eyes burning in the rain and my sight blurred. The thing stopped on a roof then and gazed down at me smiling, if you can call that a smile, like a proud parent watching its kid's marathon. Then out of nowhere, it threw something and it came flying towards me. Even before I could duck out of the way, the thing hit me on the head, sending me face first into the wet ground. A sharp pain rose in the right corner of my head, black spots obstructing my vision. Suddenly a sharp light pierced through my half closed eyelids and I felt hands, strong and rough, pull me up. I heard a lot of sound, people shouting out my name. I recognized Brianna's voice and forced my eyes open. I had hoped to see Brianna but instead I saw a man staring back at me, his eyes travelling through the surroundings and his hands around me, holding me up.

"SAM" Brianna skidded to a halt beside me, "What were you thinking?!" she said as she pulled me into a hug. I heard the others around me, their voices filled with fear and panic. Finding my voice, I said, "Brianna, you are hurting me." She let go quickly, her blue eyes full of concern.

"You are bleeding." Muriel said. She looked worn out, her black hair plastered on to her forehead, water dripping down. It was still raining but milder than before. A voice spoke up, accented, even and unfamiliar.

"Get inside."

We all looked up at the man who had held me earlier. He was motioning to a house in front of us, light pouring out of its open door. Another man stood there, a silhouette against the light.

"Didn't you hear me? Stop being a fool and get inside the house." The man said, his eyes still searching the neighborhood. I looked around me and saw a sign that indicated an address, a familiar one.

"Wait." I said, standing up, trying to remember the name from the address. "Mr.Mackendriek?" the man stared back at me, his face breaking into a grin, "It's me."

CHAPTER TWELVE

"dè an ifrinn a tha thu a 'dèanamh??" Mr.Mackendriek hurriedly pushed the six of us inside his house.

"Sorry, what?" asked Evan.

"Uh you guys are not Scottish?" asked Mr.Mackendriek. The other guy, the one that stood at the doorway, came down the steps, towels in hand. I looked down at myself. The pain in my head had not gone and I could feel a sting on the cut in my palms, might have got that when I fell. Water dripped down my clothes onto the beautifully carpeted floor and my jacket felt heavy with water.

"No, actually yes, but half Americans" replied Brianna. "Mr.Mackendriek, I am Brianna Colton. I am the daughter of Ruth and Antonio. We have met briefly a few years back. This is my brother, Samuel."

"Oh yes, yes, that's why you look so familiar" he said. "Come on, come." He walked through the doorway to the living room. The place was warm and bright, with comfortable looking chairs and a small fireplace. Everything had a Scottish touch to it, the paintings, the tapestries and even the books that lined the shelves. He handed out the towels to each one of us. "You can call me Archie. This…" he said motioning to the other guy, "… is my husband, Torence. He doesn't speak English but he does understand it."

Archie sat down inviting us to do the same. We sat huddled together on the sofa, brushing the towels on our heads.

"So, let's not pretend like we don't know what we are talking about. It will save time." He leaned forward, balancing his hands on his knees, brushing his platinum-white hair out of his eyes. "What in the world was that thing?"

We all looked at each other. So he saw it too. For a moment none of us said anything but then Muriel spoke up, "How can we trust you?"

He looked slightly amused, a smile spreading through his lips, "Well, considering that you are right now sitting in my house, dripping water everywhere, you might as well bloody trust me. Plus, your parents are just a phone call away." He said, his eyes meeting Brianna's, then mine. I knew there was no way we could get away from this.

"Mr.Mackendriek…" I began, "Archie, we don't know what that is. We saw it and out of curiosity followed it. That's it." I knew this wouldn't work as soon as I stopped talking.

"Tha sin na sgudal mòr." He stood near the doorway, leaning sideways into the wall. He was a thin man and completely in contrast to his husband with black hair and deep black eyes.

"What did he just say?" asked Aiden.

"He just said that that was a whole lot of rubbish which are exactly my thoughts too. So…" he leaned back, his eyes traveling through each of us, "…are you going to tell me the truth or are you going to continue pretending like you are just a bunch of curious little idiots?"

I noticed that I could hear music, muffled and far away but was fairly certain that it was from this house. So someone else was here too. "If we tell you the truth, will you help us? And maybe not tell our parents?" asked Muriel.

"Is there someone else in this house?" I asked.

"Damn, you ask a hell lot of questions" he exchanged a smile with Torence. "Yes we will help you, if we can and we won't tell anything to your parents and yes my sister and her husband died three years ago, so her son lives with us. Anything else?"

"No." I said.

"Then you better start talking."

*****

We took turns speaking, told them everything we knew. Archie listened intently and silently while Torence went around tending our wounds but it was evident that he was paying attention too. Finally, after we finished, Archie stared into the fireplace for some time. My wounds were neatly covered, a bandage in my hand and another one on my forehead. Brianna had one on her upper left arm and Evan had one on his palm, just like mine. The others looked wet but otherwise fine.

"And you," Archie said, fixing his eyes on me, "Thought it was brave to follow that thing? Please tell me you are out of your mind."

"I didn't want to lose it." I protested, "After all we have been through, I couldn't just let it walk…or jump away."

"Yeah Sam but you don't have to risk yourself for that." Layla said.

"Leanabh gòrach" said Torence, grinning at me.

"I am pretty sure that means that you are senseless or idiotic so I totally agree with it" said Evan, showing a thumbs up to Torence who returned it.

"Well, I have to admit that I am impressed. You lot, at such a young age, carried so much pressure and still figured out half of it." Archie said.

"So," Muriel said, "Can you help us?"

"As a matter of fact, yes I can. Actually, we can." He said, getting up. "We have both been researching on Occult studies for a long time now, so yes, maybe we can help you. We have heard about sleep paralysis, the scientific sidelines as well as the demonic ones. We can discuss about it both and figure a way out, but first of all, let's get you kids something to eat, shall we?"

"*Guid idea*", said Torence as he turned around and Archie followed him, both speaking feverishly in Scottish.

"Was it a good idea? Telling him?" asked Aiden.

"I don't know, but I have a gut feeling we can trust him." Muriel said.

"Same here." I said.

"You know what they say, trust your guts." Evan said.

"I am pretty sure it's instincts, not guts." Brianna said, smiling.

"Same thing" he said. Torence then came in and said something and left. We followed him out of the room into a dining area, hoping it was what he meant. Archie stood behind a counter, seasoning a pizza as Torence arranged plates on the table. Six for us, two for them and one for the mysterious boy with dead parents. We settled down on the table and it was not until then did I realize how hungry I felt.

"Can I use your washroom?" asked Brianna.

"Sure. Take the stairs, first door to the right." Archie said as he settled in at the head of the table. We munched down on the pizza and drank some water. The cold liquid felt amazingly cool in my throat. I heard thumping footsteps as Brianna came bursting into the room.

"THAT is your nephew?" she asked. Archie and Torence looked at each other. I heard another pair of footsteps descend down the stairs and I turned my head around to look at him. The face that came in was familiar; familiar but unpleasant.

"Florence?" asked Layla, looking like she couldn't be more pissed. "Florence Patt is your nephew?"

"Seems like you have a great reputation at school, Florence." Archie said. He was wearing a dark blue t-shirt and black shorts and half of his nose was covered in bandages. I knew I should have felt guilty but the only thing I felt was a sense of contentment. "What the hell did you do to piss these girls off?"

"Why the hell have you invited the person who broke my nose into the house?" he asked, his voice sounding different. Archie looked at him then around the table.

"Which one of you did that?" he asked.

"I did." I said slowly.

"Care to explain?" he asked, setting his pizza down.

"Well, he was being a jerk to Layla and I guess he kind of deserves it." I said.

"Well, Florence, is it true?" Archie looked at his nephew, his eyes narrowing.

"I like her." Patt said, looking at Layla then at Archie and Torence, "What's so wrong in that?"

"LIKE ME?" Layla jumped to her feet. "You made me feel insecure every time I entered school compounds, you made fun of Joceyln, even after she died and you never let go of any opportunity to make my life miserable." She turned to Archie, "Is that how the members of this family show their affection? Huh?"

"Socair sìos nighean." Archie said, pulling Layla down to her seat. "No that is not how we express our affection and I don't think that's how anyone expresses their affection." He glared at Patt "Gabh mo leisgeul"

"But…" Patt began.

"NOW" he said with a parental finality.

"I am sorry." Patt said, bending his head down.

"Is fheàrr dhut a bhith", said Torence.

"I will just grab my food and head upstairs." He said. He went over to the kitchen as Brianna settled down beside me.

*****

"There is a clear scientific explanation to sleep paralysis and then there are demonic theories." Archie said, sipping on some coffee as we ate pizza, listening intently. "Parasomnia or sleep paralysis is a medical condition that arises due to extra stress or disturbance in the sleep-wake cycle. Scientifically, it occurs when the line between sleep and wakefulness is blurred. To put it simply, you wake up while you are dreaming. As you are conscious in such a situation, you tend to hallucinate and that's just it, hallucinations. There are various versions of what people experience. Some don't see anything but only hear voices while some see different things. One is the bear you described, then there is a ghost appearance, then weird looking people roaming around."

"In Japan, it's called *kanashibari* or the magic used by monks to paralyze people. In China it's labelled ghost possession. There are many versions but the thing you saw today, that's called an Ursatimor. It's a mixture of two Latin words, 'ursa' meaning bear and 'timor' meaning fear. A bear that causes fear, to be exact."

"Hold on." Aiden said, "You knew about this thing before?"

"Why do you think I ran out of the house? To save your dumb heroic ass?" he asked, jabbing a finger at the air towards me and I blushed uncontrollably. "I ran out of the house because I saw Ursatimor and only then did I see you people. Anyway, this is not good news for us, unfortunately. Letting the Ursatimor lose is one hell of a task and trapping it back is another hell of a task."

"It's released?!" I asked. "How?"

"Well, according to myths this thing has been imprisoned for the past century or so and the source of its imprisonment is not yet clear. But it has to be released somehow, otherwise it wouldn't be here roaming around causing such *fankle*."

"Umm…praiseach?" asked Muriel.

"Praiseach means mess, kiddo." He said shaking his head as if she ought to have known that.

"So who released it?" I asked.

"And that is the first answer we need to find. That is the only way to trap this thing. We need the thing that released it to trap it back, we need something that is strong enough to hold it." We sat in silence for a long time, eating our food and thinking so hard that I thought my brains would explode.

"I know who released it." Muriel said after some time, her voice small but firm. "We did."

CHAPTER THIRTEEN

All the heads around the table turned towards Muriel as she set her pizza slice down and wiped the grease of her fingers using a tissue.

"I am sorry if it's my weird hearing, but did you just say that you *clan* released it?" asked Archie, his eyebrows rising up and staying there.

"What does *clann* mean?" asked Layla.

"The emphasis on that sentence is *obviously* on that" Archie said. "Anyway it means kids in Scottish."

"I have never heard it." she whispered.

"It's not your defective hearing Archie, I said exactly what you heard. We released it, but unknowingly." Muriel said. Her eyes travelled along the table, "Who has the Flagon?"

"What Flagon?" asked Archie.

"You think that was what happened that day?" I asked, things suddenly making sense.

"That's the most suitable explanation. It was after we opened it, that all this mess happened."

"Kids, am I missing something here?" Archie said, tapping his palms on the table. In the hurry of telling him everything, we had missed out this small part. To be honest, we had all forgotten about the Ancient Flagon until now and it was brilliant of Muriel to figure this out, taken that this was what had happened. I thought of the Flagon, sitting in my room, hiding in the shadows and if this theory was true then that Flagon was strong enough to hold the bear. We had the key and the lock.

"We came across a bottle or Flagon with ancient drawings and carvings on it that day at the church. We had opened it and then something weird happened, like the wind started blowing faster or something, but as soon as it began it ended too. We did not think it had any relevance, at least not until now" explained Aiden.

"And you conveniently forgot to mention this to me?" asked Archie.

"Yeah, why didn't you tell me?" asked Brianna.

"Wait this kiddo wasn't with you lot when all of this happened?" asked Archie.

"Tha seo troimh-chèile(''Torence said, sighing.

"Fìor" said Archie.

"And all of this you are saying makes so much sense to us." Evan said, rolling his eyes.

"Yeah, just like your adventurous account makes sense to us." Archie said. "Listen, you need to tell us everything. And when I say everything I mean *everything*, I want the whole story, you got that?" we shook our heads in unison. "Well then what are you waiting for? Open your bloody mouths people."

*****

"Ok so where is this Flagon now?"

"It's at my place. I can get it." I said. We sat around the fireplace as we talked of how we were going to trap the sleep demon- well there is something I thought I would never say. Archie and Torence had led us further than we ever did on our own. And to be truthful, it felt good having someone older involved in all of this. "So, should we go get it?" asked Aiden.

"No, not now" Archie sat up straight in his chair, resting his elbows on his knees. As he pulled his sweater sleeves down, I saw a scar that ran down the length of his right arm. "You lot need some rest. We will deal with this tomorrow. Go home, get some sleep, go to school and come over when you are free in the evening with the Flagon."

"Come on, I'll walk you out."

As we reached the door I turned around to face Archie, "Thank you, Archie. For helping us."

"Don't thank me, I think you would have figured this out even if you hadn't met me" he said, with a sly grin.

"*Tha thu uile nan clann gaisgeil agus iongantach.*" Torence said, smiling widely at all of us. I nodded at him and walked away with a sudden urge to learn Scottish.

*****

We took the long route back, finding our bikes that lay on the ground in small puddles of water, thanks to me. I walked away from the others, wanting to be alone with my thoughts. But when Muriel slowed down to walk beside me, I did not object.

"Are you ok?" she asked, her black hair cutting through her face. I slightly nodded, not knowing exactly how to answer and my thoughts drifted off.

A couple of moments later, she called impatiently. "Sam…?"

"Yeah?"

"Have you been listening to what I was saying?" she asked.

"No sorry, I zoned out. What did you say?"

"We have the Flagon, we know how to trap it but…" She said, studying the ground.

"But what?" I encouraged.

"But…we need something to trap, don't we? Where will we find it?" I had thought of that too. We had lost it once and we had seen how strong and fast that thing was. I had no idea how a bunch of teenagers and two adults were going to trap a supernatural creature like it. But instead of saying that I said, "We will find a way. We came this far, Muriel, we will do this too."

"Yeah." She pulled her mother's bizarre scarf out of a bag that slung across her shoulder and wrapped it around her neck, one hand balancing her bike. I doubted if it was the cold that made her do this.

*****

Snyder's theory on hope was the topic for my last year's assignment and so, I was well versed in it. The three components of Snyder's hope theory is one, you need to have focused thoughts, two, strategical developments and three, motivation. My thoughts were focused pretty much on one thing these days, my intention to stay alive and keep others alive was my biggest motivation, but strategy…we lacked that. I shifted on to my side and stared at the Flagon that sat on my bedside table. It looked more frightening than it looked before, the stories from its past dancing around in the dark, giving it a strange aura. I heard a slight knock on my door and heard Brianna calling me, her voice small in the looming silence. I told her that the door was open and she pushed it and walked into the room, her hands clutching onto to a piece of paper. She was wearing a plain red t-shirt and white shorts that had red hearts on it, her hair braided down her back.

"What happened?" I asked her, as she wriggled onto the bed beside me. She looked over at me, her blue eyes shining in the dark and handed me the paper she was holding. I took it from her and saw that it was a painting – of me and Morgan. Morgan was smiling at me, her hands wrapped around my waist, my hands around her shoulders. I was looking somewhere else, my lips turned up and I looked like I couldn't be happier.

"This was at my birthday." Brianna said. I turned to look at her. "My last birthday. Morgan had brought that cake and had decorated the house. That was the best birthday I ever had." Brianna was smiling.

"Yeah I remember. Morgan made me invite your friends, it was pure torture." I said, not taking my eyes off the drawing.

"I know this is a weird thing to ask to my seventeen-year old brother but can I sleep here tonight?" Brianna was blushing.

"No."

"What?" she asked, her eyes bulging out. Once I started laughing, she hit me on the head and then sank down beside me, resting her head in the crook of my arm. I pulled her closer to me, thinking of the last time we slept together - she was nine and I was ten. I was thankful she was here, happy that I had someone to get through this with, relieved to not have to sleep alone. But I did not say that aloud, instead I pulled the sheets closer towards us and closed my eyes and for the first time since Morgan's death, I slept soundly.

*****

"So", Aiden whispered, "Do you have it?"

We sat together in the last hour before lunch, hunched down in the back seats as Mr.Sattine, our Math teacher, scribbled formulae on the board. We hastily wrote down them in our notebooks. "Yeah." I said, tapping my hand on the front pocket of my bag. As soon as the bell rang, we went out towards the cafeteria and joined the others. I glanced over at the seats that used to be mine and Morgan's- it was still unoccupied.

"So are we going straight from school?" asked Brianna.

"Yeah, let's do that. I have a family dinner to attend to." Muriel said.

"What family dinner?" I asked. She let out an exasperated sigh and said, "Every week or month, we make this almost fake attempt to show that we are a closely knit family but mostly it ends up being a silent dinner with everyone heading back to our own rooms after it, as usual." I thought about the family dinners we had at home, my dad cooking dishes while mom and I set the table ready. Brianna somehow magically ends up doing nothing but eat. The thought of what Muriel lacks, pained me.

"Your father and...?" asked Layla.

"My sister, Clint." Muriel said. Layla shook her head and then took a sharp turn away from the subject, "We have two more hours until the end of school so shall we meet up at the parking lot after that?"

"Actually the last hour is history, so we are free." Aiden said.

"Cool, then I will meet you people in an hour." Evan said.

*****

"Where's Brianna?" asked Evan. He looked around us as we unlocked our bikes and got ready.

"She has class. Unfortunately her teacher did not give them a completely life changing assignment to do." said Muriel. "Don't look so disappointed, Evan."

"So, do you plan on doing it sometime soon?" I asked, as I slung my bag onto my shoulders.

"Plan on doing what?"

"Asking her out, Evan. If you haven't noticed yet, she is kind of popular in school. Don't want to lose any chances now, do we?"

"You are one hell of a supporting brother man." Evan smiled.

"Just saying." I added.

"As much as I would love to watch the brother bonding scenes, we have to get going. We can fill Brianna in later." Muriel said. We drove our way through the streets, the wind rushing by, the weather warm and cool at the same time. This was the kind of weather when the old me would settle down in our indoor garden with a book and some coffee, not go in search for creatures that could kill you and save the world. I kept my eyes on the rooftops as much as I could without tripping my bike, I wasn't ready to lose another chance at finding that thing. I could hear the Flagon moving in my bag, hitting the things around it and making a faint and consistent sound, like a strange heart, alive and evil. We reached Archie's house just as Florence parked his bike in their garage. He smiled at us, which we did not return, so he headed upstairs without saying anything. We rang the bell before getting inside, even though the door was open. Torence came and ushered us inside towards Archie who sat in the living room, his eyes fixed on the screen of his laptop, his fingers swiftly moving across the keyboard.

"So, you brought it?" he asked, pushing his platinum-white hair away from his eyes. I nodded, taking the Flagon out of my bag and placed it on the small coffee table. Torence motioned us to have a seat while Archie took the Flagon, his eyes examining every bit of it. He then handed it over to Torence, who settled down on a seat beside him. Pulling his spectacles out, he grabbed a notebook from the drawer and started taking down notes, all the while examining the Flagon with the excitement that clearly brought out the academic in him.

"What's he doing?" asked Layla.

"Torence took a two year extra course on Symbology. He knows how to figure out symbols better than anyone I have come across." Archie said with a tinge of pride in his voice.

"Oh like Robert Langdon stuff?" asked Muriel. She was Robert Langdon/ Dan Brown fan; I knew it from the repeated references she made.

"Yeah." Archie grinned, "Robert Langdon stuff." Torence turned to Archie and started talking in rapid

Scottish, indicating the drawings on the Flagon and the notes he made while Archie remained silent and attentive.

"So, he has figured something out." Archie said, as Torence got up to get a drink. "He thinks that the symbols in the Flagon depict a story and may lead us to an answer of how to trap the Ursatimor back into this. Or if it ever came from this to begin with."

"So what do we do now?" I asked.

"Now we wait."

So we waited, hours and hours as Archie browsed through his laptop, pulling up every site and article about sleep paralysis and the sleep demon while Torence sat at the table, his head bent so close to the Flagon that if he moved a little more closer, *he* could be trapped in it. All the while the six of us sat, silent and awkward. I kept texting Brianna, giving her updates but I had a fleeting feeling that Evan was doing the same thing too. After four hectic hours of doing nothing, Muriel said that she wanted to go since she couldn't miss her fake family dinner night. "I guess you all should go." Archie said. "This might take some time. Come over tomorrow after school and we will fill you in on whatever we figured out. Now go do something normal like homework."

So we left, feeling calmer and less responsible for the first time since the beginning of this bizarre and completely unwelcome adventure. It was a quiet night, with no sound other than that of the wind rushing by me as I rode my way back home. I slowed my pace and pulled my jacket closer, letting the thick material cut the cold away and just as I was starting to ride faster, my phone rang. "Yeah Brianna"

"Where are you? Evan said you guys left."

"I am on my way back. I –…"

My voice died down my throat as my eyes took in the sight in front of me. A small creature stood near the bank, hunched forward. Its face was away from me but I was certain what it was, even though I did not want to be. The Bean Nighe's long hair flew in the night wind as she bent down and washed something. I wanted to avert my eyes, look away and run from there, as far as possible and never look back. But my eyes seemed to be glued on to her and how much ever I tried, I couldn't take it away nor move a limb. Slowly, the bean nighe turned, her swollen eyes, disproportionate feet and hanging breasts coming into clear view. It was clear that she saw me but neither one of us made a move. For what felt like the longest moment of my entire life, I stood there looking at her. Then she slowly extended her right hand, a cloth clutched tight in her palm. She looked like a small kid offering something shyly to an adult, with only the clear exceptions. I did not dare to take my eyes off her but curiosity beat the fear. It was dark to properly see the cloth, so slowly I made my way near to her even though every nerve in my body wanted to do the opposite. I came within a five feet distance and as I looked down, a gasp escaped my mouth involuntarily, the fear and panic rushing through every cell of my body as I realized the cloth and who it belonged to. The red color of the scarf stood out, with tiny white and black figures on its surface – horses. I slowly walked away from her, my back completely exposed but I didn't care. I couldn't go through all of that again, this suffocating pain of loss. This time I was not going to stand there and do nothing. I lost Morgan, I wasn't losing Muriel too.

CHAPTER FOURTEEN

The end of my finger turned red as I kept it on the buzzer, the sound of the bell ringing all through the house. I knew they could hear it but I did not stop. I removed my finger away from the buzzer as the door opened and I turned to face a beautiful girl. I always knew that siblings had something or the other in common- Brianna and I had our eyes- but the resemblance between Muriel and her sister was startling. They had the same eyes and freckled face, long fingers and same body posture. Her sister did not have glasses and unlike Muriel had straight and long hair that reached till her waist. I had seen her at the prayer service but had not noticed her much.

"This is not the home of the deaf, if that's what you are looking for" she said. And there it was, yet again, the same sarcastic tone.

"I am sorry." I said, "I am looking for Muriel, I am her friend."

"Whom should I say came?" she asked.

"Sam" she left the door open as she went inside to call Muriel. I could hear the clutter of forks and knifes and small whispers from inside the house. I kept my eyes fixed on the rooftops, my heart beating much faster than it was supposed to. After a minute or so, Muriel came out, wearing a worried look on her face that scared the hell out of me. "What's wrong?" we both asked at the same time.

"Are you ok?" I asked her.

"Unlike you, yeah I am ok. What's wrong Sam?"

I didn't hear the rest of anything she said as I let out a sigh of relief and pulled her into a hug, cutting her off from whatever she was saying. "You are ok." I whispered.

"Sam." she said, pulling me away and fixing me with a strong gaze. "You are freaking the hell out of me. What is going on?"

I stood there not knowing what to say. But somewhere deep down, I knew that not telling her was more dangerous than telling her. So I took hold of her hand and pulled her out into the lawn, where there were a pair of chairs and a table, saying. "We need to talk."

*****

"Muriel?"

She sat there, rigid and stiff, her eyes fixed somewhere far beyond as if that could give a solution. I had tried to put it as mildly as possible but I was never good at words. And one never knows the pain of loss until you stare at it in the face. I looked at Muriel, the first ever person I felt close to after Morgan. And surprising both of us, I said, "What do you want to be?"

"What?" she looked at me, speaking for the first time since I had finished speaking.

"What do you want to be Muriel?"

"I don't know…alive?" she said, a small grin tugging at her lips. I shook my head, "You know what I mean."

"Well, I wanted to be a doctor."

"Wanted?" I asked.

"Yeah, I don't want to anymore. I want to start a band" she said.

"Wait, you sing?" I asked. She shook her head slightly and said, "Yeah. I can play a few instruments too." A sudden resolve filled my insides.

"Can you sing something for me?" I asked.

"Now?"

"No" I said, getting up. She got up too and we walked over to her house. "When all of this is over."

She didn't say anything for a while but then looked at me, her eyes distant and far. "I want you to promise me something." When I did not say anything, she continued, "I want you to not tell anyone about this."

"What?!"

"Please Sam. This is our only chance. You can't tell them, at least not until I tell you to." She looked at me pleadingly, her hands squeezing my fingers so much so that they hurt.

"And when is that?"

"When it's time, you will know."

*****

Muriel had to push me out of the house for me to go, like literally. I had a feeling that leaving her there alone was a bad idea. But multiple calls from Brianna and my parents led me back home. The house was fully lit when I parked my bike and I knew I was in trouble. Even though I knew everyone was awake, I slowly made my way across the yard and into the house. As I shut the door behind me with a squeak, a voice filled the silent house.

"Samuel, come here!"

I slowly walked towards my dad's sound and ended up at the dining area. Brianna, mom and dad sat at one side of the table, facing the door, the two pairs of blue eyes and a pair of hazel ones staring at me. I sat down opposite them without another word, like a criminal waiting for his verdict.

"Where were you?" asked my dad.

"I…" I looked over at Brianna but she looked at me with so much anger that I could have burned up then and there. I knew that my parents wanted me to have a normal life, with good grades, lots of friends and a great girlfriend. So I said, "I was with Muriel." which *was* true.

"Muriel? Who is that?" asked my mom. I knew my strategy had worked, I just needed one last touch.

"She is my…" the long pause, the master stroke, "… friend."

"Ok." My dad said, after exchanging a look with my mom, "But this is not acceptable anymore, if you are going to be late, then show some responsibility and inform us or your sister."

"Yes." I said, "I am sorry, my bad."

"Well then, go get some sleep. Good night."

I murmured a goodnight and slowly got up from the table when mom called, "Sam, honey."

"Yeah, mom."

"Can we meet this Muriel sometime?"

Oh no, I thought but I said, "Yeah sure" and ran my way up the stairs. As I reached the handle to my door, Brianna came up behind me. "Care to give an explanation?"

"I told you" I said, "I was with Muriel." she looked unconvinced so I said, "You can ask her if you want."

"Wait, so are you guys…"

"No no no no no nah." I said, "She just wanted to blow off some heat." I said. "After the whole "family dinner" stuff." Brianna just shook her head and then went to her own room. I went to mine, locking the door behind me, something I hadn't done since I brought Brianna into this mess. I kicked my shoes off, and sent a text to Muriel, making sure she was alright. And then I lay down on my bed and cried, the tears flowing effortlessly from my eyes. I felt confident that I could do something, anything to stop this, to end this tangled up mess. I thought that this was it, no more pain, no more loss, no more lies, just more answers and solutions. But here I was again, way back to where it all had begun. I hate this life, this process of cleaning up, one after the other, burning the mistakes and fears, just to see the ashes reforming and then burning them down again. And one day, the flame that is supposed to burn the fears down, burns our fragile lifeline but its ashes don't reform, instead we go away, as dust and memories.

*****

"So, we figured out what this meant." Archie said, his fingertips travelling through the carved surface of the Flagon. Torence and the rest of us sat around the table, paying close attention. "These carvings you see here, those small figures denote people and over here" he said moving his finger from one corner to another, "That shows the Ursatimor. At the back of the Flagon, you see a small carving that looks exactly like this bottle. And the figures after this do not contain the demon, which means that..."

"They locked it up." Brianna finished. Archie shook his head in agreement, "Briefly, this shows the story of a village full of people who were attacked by the demon.

They managed to trap it in this bottle centuries ago. But there is more to it than we thought."

"What do you mean?" I asked. 'More to it' was not exactly what we needed.

"The village this story takes place in is Waltunor."

"What?! Here?" Evan asked, looking at Archie and then at all of us. To be frank, I was not surprised. "How do you know that?"

"There is a Scottish inscription on the inside of the cap that states the time and the date. We did some digging and we found out something. You must have heard this story in different forms, as legends and myths or even bedtime stories. Only a couple of people knew about this demon that caused destruction, so they gathered and met in places without others knowing. But the more we try to hide something, the more visible it becomes. Other uninvolved people started referring to them as a cult or demonic worship group. From here on the story is kind of a blur. They say that these people tried to lock the demon in a church, as it is a holy place but then things went wrong somehow and everyone on that spot that day died."

"La Iglesia de Muerta por Dentro" murmured Layla.

"Sorry, what?" asked Archie.

"The church you mentioned now. I have heard this story. That's where we found the Flagon."

"And released the demon" Muriel added.

"So, does that mean…" Brianna eyed each of us carefully.

"That we began all of this mess? Yeah, pretty much." I said. I looked over at Muriel but she kept her eyes fixed on her hands. Ever since last night, she seemed withdrawn and silent and I wasn't the only one who noticed it, although the others blamed it on the pretend family dinner and not the death sword that hung above her head. "So what do we do?" I ask because we had to do something.

"Below the name and date there is another inscription. It sounds like a spell, might be something to trap the demon but I am not sure it will work." Torence said through Archie.

"It's not like we have any other strong leads." Brianna said, with so much finality and confidence that I wanted to believe her, believe that this could be the end. "Let's do this."

"Yeah kiddo but we have one major drawback. We don't know where the Ursatimor is."

"I do." Muriel said. All heads turned towards her as she lifted her eyes to meet mine and I knew it was time, now or never. "Don't ask me anything more. Tonight, Sam will lead you to my house and you all will know what to do." With that she stormed out of the room. I looked around the table as the meaning of her words sank in on each of them. I quickly stood up and started following Muriel down the hall. I shouted her name as she stood there in the lane, unlocking her bike. Even if she heard me, she didn't respond, so I ran up to her.

"Sam, please go back. You know what to do."

"You keep saying that." I said, my voice rising by every word. "I don't know what to do Muriel. I don't. You can't just put this all on me and walk away."

And then she was shouting back, "Yes I can because the alternate scares the hell out of me. If I don't do that then I will have to stand here and accept my death when for the first time I have so much to live for." And then as a whisper she said, "And I can't do that."

She climbed onto her bike and rode away, leaving me to stand there, her words echoing inside me, 'I can't do that'. Neither can I.

*****

"We know you knew Sam."

Brianna laced her fingers through mine, as we sat on my bed, the rest on the floor. "Why didn't you tell us anything?"

"Because she told me not to. She thought you would try to stop her."

"Hell yeah we would. She can't just die on us." Evan said.

"How did you know it was her?" asked Aiden.

"I saw the bean nighe with Muriel's mom's scarf" my voice sounded hollow. We sat around the room in silence and I knew that none of us were ready for this, we weren't prepared for another loss.

"So that's it? We are just going to sit here and let that thing take her away from us?" Brianna said, getting up.

"No, we can't let that happen." Layla said and after some time she added. "We'll find a way. I need to make some calls."

"Use my room." Brianna said. As Layla opened the door, she let out a yelp as she walked straight into Muriel. We all stood up and I wondered what made Muriel come back.

"I just want to…" Muriel began, "I…Mmm…I am sorry."

"For what?" asked Evan, "For being you? The last time I checked that wasn't something you apologized for."

Muriel smiled her beautiful smile then dropped her bag onto the bed and sat down, I sat on the floor while Layla and Brianna sat on the bed. "I freaked out and I shouldn't have."

"You have every reason to." added Evan.

"Just because I am going to die, you don't have to go soft on me Miles."

"My bad."

Muriel laughed. Then she fished into her bag and pulled out a pen drive, "If things go terribly wrong tonight, then I want you guys to watch a video in this. You will find it in a folder named bean nighe."

"Creative name, where did you find it?" Brianna grinned.

"I have my sources" she said.

"When you mean terribly wrong, do you mean when you come back out alive or…" Evan asked. Muriel threw a pillow at him and he dodged out of the way. She tried to meet my eyes but this time I was the one avoiding it. We talked for a while and it was hard to believe that things could go bad, that these people could feel anything other than happiness. After a while, Layla went to make some calls (whatever that meant) and Brianna went to make us some coffee. Evan followed her, as expected, and Aiden, seeing that things are getting awkward, got up and followed Evan to the kitchen. Seeing that Muriel and I were the only ones in the room, I got up to leave too.

"Sam." When I didn't stop she said, "Is this how you really want to remember the last few minutes we spend together?"

"No." I said, turning around, "Because this is not the last few minutes we are spending together Muriel. You are not going to die."

"Sam" she said again, as if saying my name could change everything. "If this is how it is meant to end, then it should end that way. It is what it is Sam."

"How do you know its tonight? How do you know that it will come tonight?" I asked.

"Because that's what happened with Morgan and Jocelyn and everyone else." Seeing that I was not at all convinced, she said, "Sam, we don't have another solution."

"Don't tell me you don't have a little bit of hope that you will survive this."

"I have hope." She whispered.

"Then that's all that matters. You are not dying on me." I said, jabbing my finger in the air. For a moment she just stood there and looked at me, tears flowing easily down her freckled cheeks. I slowly walked over to her, pulling her into a hug, her sobs echoing in my small room. She untangled herself from me after some time, pulling me to the ground with her. She sat with her legs crossed over, her hands wiping the tears away and then she closed her eyes and started singing.

"Deep, deep down,

I had lost my home.

To weather and time,

I had lost my home."

"The tears and happiness,

Fought wars that never end,

As I lost my home,

To love and hope."

Her face turned peaceful and relaxed, her voice so different and sweet. I looked at her, astonished, at the lines near her eyebrows that moved as she sang. She remained like that for some time, eyes closed, calm and peaceful.

"I don't want to die on you" she said as she slowly opened her eyes, "But it's not like I have a choice."

"You always have a choice." I whispered. When she didn't say anything I asked, "Do you trust me?"

Her hands tightened around mine and after a small silence, she said, "I do."

"We need to talk."

*****

Layla pulled us all to the indoor garden just as mom and dad came home. We gathered around the room as Layla spoke in one breath.

"I called Torence and told him to check up on the previous deaths. He had access to some authorities and he found out something that might actually be our loophole." She paced around the room, her hands pressed together so tightly that her knuckles looked white. "He got the postmortem reports of the previous deaths. Apparently, they all died due to lung and rib fracture which led to lack of air in the thoracic chamber. Scientifically, these cause instant death but we are not here to talk science. I guess this fracture happens when the bear sits on the person and exerts force but it does something that delays the death for as long as 24 hours, from what we have seen."

"And how exactly is this helpful for us?" asked Brianna.

"I am coming to that point. But do you guys have any doubts?"

"How in the world did you talk to Torence?" asked Muriel.

"For a person who might die within a few hours, that's a stupid thing to ask. But my grandmother was full Scottish so I can speak the language, but not fluently." Layla stood in the middle of the room, hands on her hips, her hair flying in the slight breeze. "Ok, now comes the important part. What if we stop the bear before it causes the damage?"

"What do you mean?" I asked.

"If we trap the bear before it can damage the ribs or lungs then Muriel does not have to die. Even if she sustains minor breakage, she can survive it." Her eyes shone so bright, with possibility and more than that, hope. I looked over at Muriel and saw the slightest hint of hope pass through her eyes.

"That's amazing Layla." Aiden said.

"Wait." Muriel said, "Layla you have a brilliant plan and trust me when I say that I want it to work more than anyone else but if you can't stop the demon before it hurts me, promise me that you won't let it go."

"Muriel…"

"Promise me." she said. "All of you. If I survive without trapping the demon, I will never forgive you all." Everyone kept quiet, no one saying anything and so I said, "I promise."

CHAPTER FIFTEEN

"Sam."

I turned around to find my mom sitting on the sofa, her legs spread out on the coffee table. She had a book in her hand, which she placed carefully on her lap as she beckoned me towards her.

"Yeah?"

"The girl that just left…was that Muriel?" my mom asked, trying to keep her voice casual but completely failing. I nodded my head in approval, not sure what to say. "She's pretty."

"Yeah, she is."

"So why did she leave so soon?"

Because there is a good chance that she might get killed by a sleep demon today, so I said, "She has to run some errands."

*****

It had been an hour since Muriel left. We sat around in the indoor garden, an ominous silence hanging in the air. Aiden sat near the railing, his legs hanging down between the rods. Layla kept glancing at her phone and Evan and Brianna sat in silence, her hands in his. Seeing them together, I felt lonely, like I was behind an invisible wall that cut me off from the rest of the world. After one long hour of silence, Layla's phone rang. She hastily answered it and turned towards us, "It's time."

*****

We took our positions around Muriel's house, completely covering all sides of the entrance. Archie, Brianna and I stood at the rear in darkness, jumping at any movement or sound. There was a ladder, leaning against the wall, ready to lead us to Muriel, its silver paint shining in the dark. Archie wore a casual t-shirt, his scar clearly visible even in the night. "What happened?" I asked, before I could think it through. Anything to take my mind off the present situation.

"I was in the vehicle when my sister's car hit the side of a bridge and fell down into the water." he said, his eyes fixed on the light that came from a room upstairs, Muriel's room. "I knew how to swim, so I took Florence with me too, but when I went back for my sister and her husband…it was too late."

"I am sorry." Brianna said.

"You shouldn't be. You didn't do anything." Archie grinned. I thought about him and Torence and even Florence, the loss of their family haunting them, about Evan, Layla, Brianna and Aiden, the pain they all went through, about Muriel, about what she has lost and what she might lose now. About me and everything I felt. I was filled with a sudden resolve to not let anything like that happen to anyone anymore.

"Holy shit." whispered Archie. I followed his line of vision, and saw a shadow looming over in the light at Muriel's room, a shadow faintly human. The Ursatimor, my brain provided. We looked at each other, Archie furiously texting someone, probably Torence and pulled the Flagon out. He started climbing the ladder and I followed, Brianna at my heels. I heard footsteps below me, the skin of my palms wet with sweat. Archie jumped in through the window, moving out of sight, followed by Brianna and then me. I almost lost my balance but Archie caught me, a finger at his lips, eyes fixed somewhere behind me. I turned around silently as Brianna helped the others in through the window and saw that we were at the far right corner of a large room. The walls were white, filled with posters of bands like One Direction and The Beatles and a large bookstand near the window we had jumped in through. The bed was in the center and in it lay Muriel, small inside the comforter and on her sat the Ursatimor. For a second, none of us moved, not exactly sure how to make the first move. The thing sat on her, its back to us, silent and unmoving and this close I could see the long nails in what looked like fingers and the red-brown hair that covered every inch of its body. Archie slowly walked over to the bed, as silently as he could, whispering something under his breath. The demon tensed, as if it sensed danger, the muscles in its back flexing and slowly turned its head to face us. It shifted in position, now completely facing us and Muriel let out a small groan. "Do it." I whispered. "Do it Archie, NOW."

Archie took a deep breath, unscrewed the bottle and began

"O sgriosadair anaman,

reul a 'bhàis,

cuir a-steach don bhotal naomh seo

agus fàg sinn mar,

tha mi ag àithneadh *dhut!"*

The creature let out a howl of pain, so piercing that I found myself automatically covering my ears.

"O sgriosadair anaman,

reul a 'bhàis,

cuir a-steach don bhotal naomh seo

agus fàg sinn mar,

tha mi ag àithneadh *dhut!"*

Archie was now practically screaming. He repeated the verse again and again as the demon cried in pain and then it dug its finger nails into the comforter. Muriel screamed at the top of her lungs, a scream that chilled me to the core of my bones. Archie did not stop and the creature dug further into her. "NO!!!" I screamed as I ran forward.

A pair of big arms pulled me back and however hard I tried, I couldn't break free.

"*Na dèan, a mhic*" Torence whispered in my ears, as he held me back. I squeezed my eyes shut, relying on my hearing, the sounds of pain and loss cutting its way into me. I could hear Archie shouting, Muriel screaming and the rest of us crying, the sobs heartbroken and painful. The demon let out one last scream and I heard a swish of a sound and then silence. I stopped struggling against Torence who let go immediately. I wanted to stay there and never open my eyes but I knew I had to and as I slowly opened it, the first thing that I registered was the blood, her blood. I ran over to the bed, almost slipping on the blood that covered the floor in a pool.

"Muriel." I called out to her as I shook her. Her eyes remained closed, the color fading from her face with every passing second, her lips dark and her hair lose. Her t-shirt was covered in blood and it was still flowing out of her, taking her life with it. "No, please, MURIEL." I tried to cover the wound, stop the blood from flowing but it flew through my fingers as if nothing could stop it. I screamed my throat raw, my hands shaking uncontrollably, my heart breaking to a million small pieces. "Do you trust me?" I had asked her.

"I do." She had told me and I wasn't able to help her. Not now, not ever. I could see black spots covering my vision, the darkness slowly growing inside me. And somewhere in between darkness and pain, I was led away from her.

CHAPTER SIXTEEN

Two weeks. It's been two weeks since the last time I went out of this house, last time I slept properly, last time I saw Muriel or any of the others. The funeral was the day after the incident and as her father and sister were out, we didn't have to do much explaining, also we left no signs to show our presence there. The sounds weren't heard by anyone in the lone neighborhood and none of us had any idea how that was possible but we had had enough mysteries for a lifetime now. With some help, Muriel's death was pushed aside as an accidental one, what kind of accident…I don't know. I never planned on finding out either. Archie told me that everything was taken care of, that they had trapped the demon and that no more deaths would come our way. "This is what she wanted." Of course it is.

*****

"Sam? Are you in there?" I swung my legs out of my bed and walked over and opened the door. I expected to see just Brianna but I found Archie and Torence with her too. "Hope we aren't disturbing you." Archie said. I assured them that they weren't disturbing me as it had been two weeks since I had actually done something. We walked down to the living room as my parents were at work so we could talk openly. "I am sorry, both of you." Archie said. I didn't say anything so he continued, "I came here to tell you something."

"What is it?" asked Brianna. She looked different, tired and weak.

"She knew." Archie said after exchanging a look with Torence.

"What do you mean?" I asked.

"She knew she wasn't going to make it. She knew the dangers of trapping it while it was still on her but she was adamant that we do it."

We sat in silence, my mind nothing but a blank page. After some time Archie and Torence got up to leave and just before leaving Torence looked at me and said, "*Tha tòrr a bharrachd agad airson a bhith beò.*"

I looked over at Archie, confused and he said, "He said that you have so much more to live for. And right it is, my son."

*****

The six of us sat in Evan's bedroom as it was the only one with a TV. Evan connected the pen drive as I sat in silence, staring out of the window. He scrolled through the files until he came across the file named 'bean nighe'. He turned towards us, "Shall I play it?"

This was it, I thought. The last piece of Muriel in this world, nothing more left. I could feel the hesitation in each of us but finally Brianna said, "Go ahead, Evan."

Muriel's face came into view. She wore a black t-shirt that said, 'Who doesn't love chocolate?' her eyes bright and shining, her red lips pulled into that beautiful smile of hers, her bushy black hair completely down in curls around her shoulder. "If you are seeing this, then I guess things didn't end well. I am sorry for your loss" she began, her face turning happy at her own joke. "Everyone has a destined life span on this earth and mine was just smaller than yours. It's not your fault that you get to live more than me and even if we hadn't met, I believe that I could have died around this time. Maybe not by a demon but that sounds like a cool way to die. But before I say anything else, I want you guys to know something."

"I knew. I knew that I wasn't going to make it and that's exactly why I am sure that you guys are seeing this now. I was afraid of death and leaving all this behind until that moment." She hesitated. "After Sam left that night, I went for a ride, partly to think and partly because I was too afraid to sleep. And I found myself at the bank of river Fleei, don't ask me how because I don't know and I saw the bean nighe there too. But it didn't have my scarf with it. Instead it had the dress I wore to Rease's funeral. I thought that just confirmed things, that my death was sure, until I realized who the dress actually belonged to."

Brianna let out a small gasp and I turned to find the tears falling down in full speed. I wanted to reach for her hand but I was too stunned to move.

"Brianna, you are one of the most amazing people that I have ever met. The world needs you, your parents need you, and your brother needs you. So I couldn't let that happen. And don't beat yourself up over this, it's not your fault, it never was. And don't think that your decision on not believing was the problem. The real problem isn't the lack of faith, it is the presence and over importance of it."

"Evan, you are a great guy. You have nothing to be afraid of…except maybe your temper, although I highly suspect that's something other people should be afraid of. But get those guts in order and ask Brianna out. If you haven't yet, then I just made things easier for you. Happy I could help."

"Layla, you don't have Jocelyn anymore to kick bully asses but you have us, at least them. But you don't need other people because you are completely and fully capable of it yourself and I knew it the moment I saw you shouting at Archie about Florence. Be strong, you need that in this world."

"Aiden, you are a brilliant guy. You will one day become famous for that big brain of yours; just don't shrink into yourself like you normally do. You have them and trust me, that is all you need."

"Sam" I felt my heart beating inside my chest, so fast and so hard that I thought the others could hear it. "I know that you haven't done anything since this happened, that you shut yourself off from everything and remained closed in that small room of yours. Don't do that anymore. You are a great person and I wish I could have spent more time with you but that's not in our hands. I trust you more than anyone and I want you to move forward. So get up and go get an ice cream if it will help you "cool down"" she laughed.

"So, I guess that's it. I have never felt more at home than I have felt with you all. Thank you, for accepting me for who I am and for loving me despite everything. I hope you cried like hell at my funeral." She laughed again. "Goodbye, you all."

"Oh and don't forget to submit the assignment."

And with that she was gone but not exactly gone.

EPILOGUE

"This looks excellent" Mr.Beckham said.

"Thank you" we all said in unison.

"Can you tell me the names of all the members?"

"Samuel Colton." Evan began.

"Layla Beckett" Mr.Beckham scribbled furiously onto the paper.

"Evan Miles"

"Aiden Hunter"

"Muriel Payton"

We walked out of the classroom, leaving the assignment behind but carrying everything else along with us.

THE END